ALSO BY JOHN EDGAR WIDEMAN

The Homewood Trilogy

Look for Me and I'll Be Gone: Stories

You Made Me Love You: Stories

American Histories: Stories

Writing to Save a Life: The Louis Till File

Fanon: A Novel

Briefs: Stories for the Palm of the Mind

God's Gym: Stories

The Island: Martinique

Hoop Roots: Basketball, Race, and Love

Two Cities: A Novel

The Cattle Killing: A Novel

Fatheralong: A Meditation on Fathers and Sons, Race and Society

All Stories Are True

The Stories of John Edgar Wideman

Philadelphia Fire: A Novel

Fever: Stories

Reuben: A Novel

Brothers and Keepers: A Memoir

Sent for You Yesterday: A Novel

Damballah: Stories

Hiding Place: A Novel

The Lynchers: A Novel

Hurry Home: A Novel

A Glance Away: A Novel

SLAVEROAD

JOHN EDGAR WIDEMAN

SCRIBNER

New York London Toronto Sydney New Delhi

Scribner
An Imprint of Simon & Schuster, LLC
1230 Avenue of the Americas
New York, NY 10020

First Scribner hardcover edition October 2024

Interior design by Kyle Kabel

Manufactured in the United States of America

1 3 5 7 9 10 8 6 4 2

Library of Congress Cataloging-in-Publication Data has been applied for.

ISBN 978-1-6680-5721-6
ISBN 978-1-6680-5723-0 (ebook)

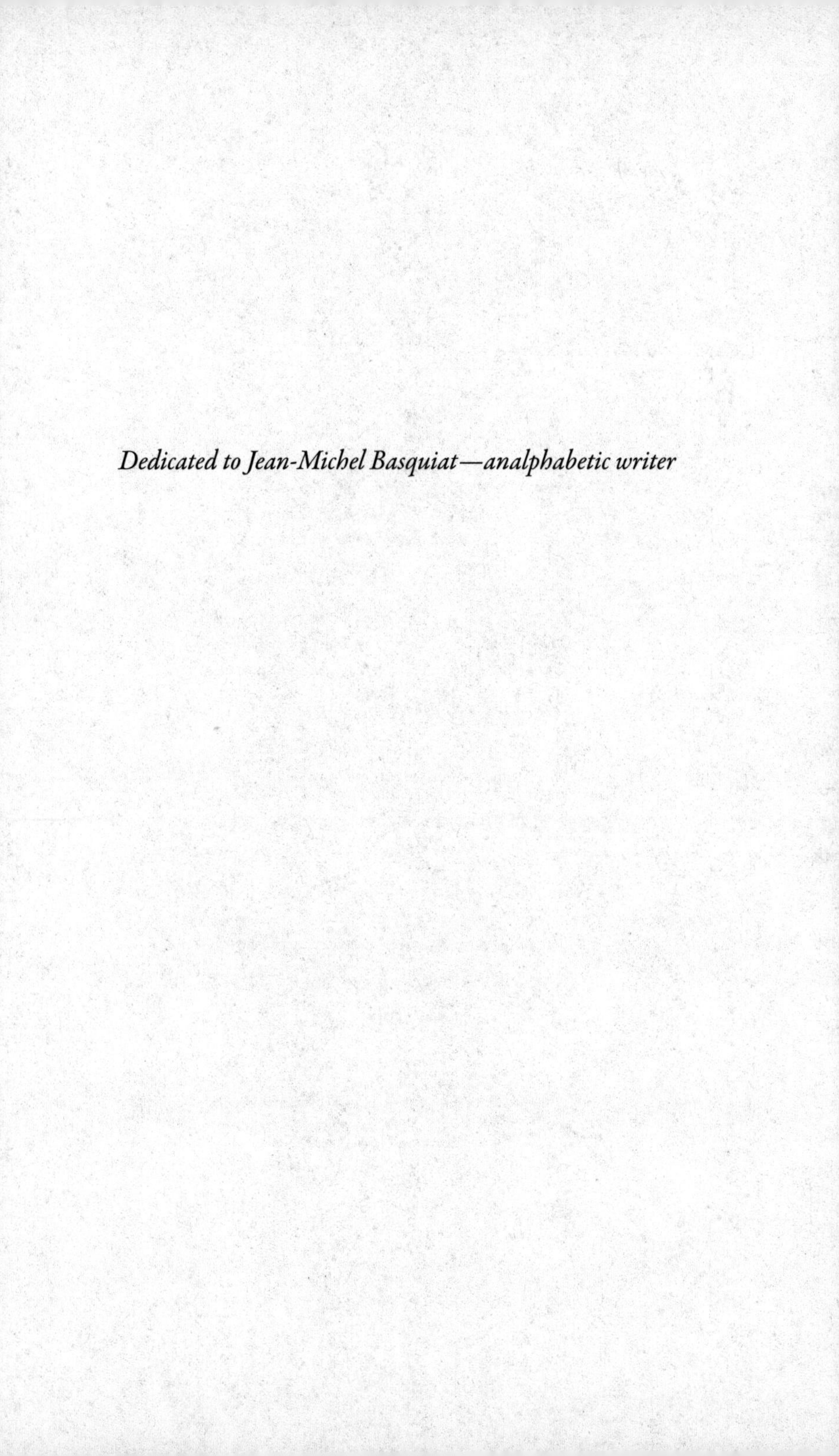

Dedicated to Jean-Michel Basquiat—analphabetic writer

CONTENTS

CONTENTS

AUTHOR'S FOREWORD

I'm trying hard and failing to find words to say to my son, who has been awake most of the night in the emergency ward of a North Carolina hospital where his mother, my wife for thirty-two years until we divorced two decades ago, lies dying. Morning now where my son is, and he tells me his mother has survived and been transferred back to the senior-citizens care facility in which, despite her protests, her anger, her insistence she's quite capable of taking care of herself, it has been necessary to commit her involuntarily for the past year while various illnesses ravaged her and she rapidly deteriorated physically and mentally. He tells me that after the frantic, exhausting, frightening ordeal of the ER, she appeared peaceful when he finally left her at dawn. A shower, a call to me, and he'll return to her bedside in a room set up for hospice care. His mother off cumbersome life support now, heavily sedated, and he hopes she will remain pain free and calm for the hours or day or few days at most the doctors guess she may have left. But she's still fighting, my heart knows Mom's still fighting, my son says. Mom always a fighter. And I nod and agree, *yes, oh yes,* listening intently to my son's voice coming from the phone. But I find I have nothing to say. Only ghosts of words. A suffocating, mocking flock of them, too little, too late, like any words I could summon up and say now to his mother, words that would trivialize both her and myself, words that would only demean our long, long separation, our long silence, if suddenly I found myself transported, standing at her bedside.

As hard to find words of support for my son today, on this particular morning for him that is a late afternoon for me, here across the ocean in France; as hard, hard to find words as it is sometimes when I'm speaking to my other son, my son's younger brother, a prisoner in Arizona for over thirty years, beginning at age sixteen, until five years ago he was granted probation by the Arizona Board of Executive Clemency and released. Probation the board then chose for its own unreasonable reasons to promptly rescind after only nine months, re-incarcerating my son perhaps forever, the board free to never release him again since it has been granted absolute power by the laws of the state of Arizona. The power to be sole judge, jury, and executioner of inmate rights. Including an inmate's right, following probation, to due process guaranteed by the United States Constitution. The board privileged not to be answerable to any other authority—legal, moral, ethical, on earth or otherworldly. Or rather, to put it another way, about as answerable at this moment as death is answerable to my elder son as he shepherds his mother through her final hours.

So I find myself with nothing to say. Except unbearable words I cannot dare to speak to him or myself. Except this autobiography, this fiction, these silent words I imagine and write. Imagined like the better me I wish I could imagine myself to be. In a world unimaginably different and better than this one we inhabit. *Oh yes. Yes.* A fighter.

My son's worried. Voice pinched, out of breath. Anxious to return to his mother, so no way he's going to allow an awkward pause, this slowing down of back-and-forth in an impossible conversation, to last one second more than it should. Too much at stake, too much to do. He's not going to risk the unthinkable consequence of missing her final moments. Nothing I might say or anybody else might say worth suffering that loss. He knows it. I know it. Hurries off the line—*Wish us luck, Dad.* Emptiness, clutter of empty words rattles in a space between us now neither one understands how to fill.

We are mixed. All of us human beings mixed. Mixtures of everything unknown and known, inside or outside of us, or wherever else anything resides. What passes through us. Or what we pass through. Mixtures languages try to define with words. Words separating one thing, one moment from another. Words separating each one of us from the other one. Separating languages each person speaks. Each of us alone in vast silence beyond words. Beyond any language anyone speaks.

I considered titling this book—*Slaveroad: An Autobiography*. I still sometimes think that should be the title. If a man named Otto wrote a book about his life, would you call it an Otto biography. Or would you call it an autobiography. Wouldn't Otto's book be both. Or neither. Otto's book simply Otto's book unless you let someone distract you with silly wordplay. A dumb pun. A sound mixing up sameness and difference. But oddly enough, whatever you choose to call Otto's book—poetry, novel, history, fiction, biography, holy writ, etc.—or call this book or any book before you pick it up to read it, can change the meaning of words printed on the book's pages.

My name's not Otto. Though, like Otto, I am a character, an author being imagined as he writes himself. Step by step. Going along to get along. Telling (and retelling) a story about his life. (Fiction/autobiography.) As word follows word, I am no more, no less make-believe than the character Otto I proposed above.

My fictional Otto with a fictional book he's written about himself—his Otto biography or autobiography—bears, like me, no color I have named. If I wish readers to believe Otto is real and to pay attention to him, to me, should I attach a color to Otto and to myself. Don't readers expect writers, sooner or later, in one fashion or another, to indicate the color of characters. Should I give Otto's color a name. Name my color. Doesn't color hover impatiently, inevitably, as each life story that we read or write commences. Color offstage perhaps, but forever anxious to be introduced. To assert an unavoidable presence.

Perhaps you have already chosen a color to call me. To call these words, this book, this life I'm imagining with you. This life shared in our heads, under our feet, while our bodies borne on a slaveroad created long, long ago and still here moment by moment while I, while you, ask questions about the color of characters who may or may not exist. Am I obliged (is my writing compelled) to attach color to people if I wish readers to believe that characters I'm writing about are actual people. People like them. Real. People with a color that separates and distinguishes one kind of person from another. People whose color is always part of any story pretending to be true.

To give weight (reality) to my words, to my story—and it's always my story no matter what else the words seem to be—must my story, any story, identify and confirm presumptions of color that exist in a reader's understanding. Expectations already formed, unshakable conclusions about who she or he or they are. Understandings imposed, in place for uncountable centuries before you begin reading even a single word of this story I'm imagining.

The words that follow are hoping to discover a different starting place. To ask how any person gets here. Ask the meaning of getting here, and what happens next. Words chasing the most ancient, most elusive storyline, far older than this slaveroad we ride. Words seeking to mirror time passing. Lost time. Implacable, uncolored time. Words pretending to spin time—that most familiar, least resolvable narrative—from air.

I don't intend this book to be a confession. Confessions, when delivered voluntarily, imply sharing. Imply secrets, surprises, revelations of concealed and possibly incriminating information. *Confession* suggests the possibility of expanding mutual intimacy and trust. Confession may be driven by a wish, a desire, perhaps, to do better. Admirable intentions even on a slaveroad. Any confession I might offer starts with a confession: like you—my readers, my fellow sufferers—in this autobiography I am writing of a man on a slaveroad, I am incorrigible.

To any intelligent soul, this narrative and what it may reveal about me won't be shocking, and certainly no revelation. I stink, bleed, lie, fear life and death almost equally, disguise myself from others, divide myself from others and from myself, have perpetrated unforgivable, grievously damaging acts that have injured uncountable strangers as well as the very few individuals whom I profess to love. These facts don't separate me from my kind. So what's to confess. Any observant, twenty-first-century citizen of the world is familiar already with the truth that you or I, any and all of us, including our designated leaders and saints, are capable of participating in the worst sorts of low-down, dirty, nasty, despicable business. All of us members of the unkind kind we entitle humankind. Unkind to one another. Unkind to every environment we inhabit.

Our unkind kind has demonstrated a willingness, even an eagerness, to do evil unto others. As if doing evil to others of our kind might preserve us from evil our kind would, if offered an opportunity, do unto us.

Hurt, subdue, and dominate others before they have a chance to hurt, subdue, and dominate you. Isn't that the golden rule of survival. Understood bone deep, unequivocally, and practiced always whether we speak the rule aloud or not. Be cunning, lay low when necessary, and seem to offer no threat. But always be prepared to strike. Strike first if possible. Quickly, with irresistible force.

We have become at least as adept at destroying fellow humans as we are at nurturing and protecting humankind. We invented African slavery. Waged wars to kidnap Africans from their villages and force-march them in chains to fortified depots established by Europeans along the West African coast. Prisoners warehoused there until packed into ships that sailed across the Atlantic Ocean to a so-called New World of colonies and settlements Europeans were rapidly developing on Caribbean islands in Central, South, and North America.

The absolute power of their captors to torture and murder them compelled Africans to obey the dictates, desires, the will of those who had stolen them and consigned them to lifelong servitude. Submit or die was the choice passed on, generation after generation, to the offspring of Africans who had endured the pain, punishment, and horror of captivity.

The death of the last legally enslaved person didn't stop the institution of slavery from continuing to proliferate. It has taken me many years to learn that simple fact, and would require many more lifetimes to express just how grievously I am still affected. Slavery's consequences resonate in our daily lives, our personal and cultural memories. Slavery is kept alive by old and new suffering generation after generation. Suffering and pain passed on as riches are passed on by the rich to the rich.

Whether or not direct descendants of slaves, we all inherit the curses of slavery because we practice and embrace in our language, our personal habits, our social and governmental institutions, the idea that color not only identifies African ancestry but also signifies an intrinsic, unchanging difference in worth between some lives and others.

Color separates forever, we still believe. Still believe we are Coloreds and Whites. Two different colors distinguishing separate kinds and orders of human life. With such thinking we resurrect moment by moment, day after day the rationalizations that created enslaved and enslavers. Condemn our kind to be eternally both. Eternal slaves of a version of ourselves we invented when we invented enslavement.

What greater crimes lurk offstage, in the wings, awaiting a turn on this slaveroad. And confession or not from me, we are, you and I, already complicit. Guilty of aiding and abetting whatever crimes lie ahead.

WHO IS SHEPPARD

If asked to tell his story, what would William Henry Sheppard say. Dead now all these years. Nothing. He says nothing and I listen. Words begin. Pages turn.

Sheppard stares at the sea saying nothing day after day. Cold, cold ocean is what he sees. One more river to cross. Or a boundless expanse. Africans chained deep in the ship's deep, black belly. If he asked them to tell their story, what would they say. Dead so long. And soon he, too, will be dead. Nothing then. Crying in the building soon be over, soon be over.

The dark ships move / the dark ships move, a poet will write. Passengers and cargo sailing across a cold sea. Cargo and passengers. When the ships dock, somebody will be in charge and separate one from the other: cargo from passengers. Captain, crew, passengers separated from cargo.

Color separates, the ones in charge decree. Now and forever after, they decree. Color, they decree, separates cargo from passengers. Magic, they decree. Now you see color, now you don't, but color forever, they decree. Color and separation understood as a single word. You can't say one without saying the other. You cannot see, cannot mean one without meaning the other. Color and separation as inseparable as cold and sea.

Whale-road, the bards called the sea, whale-road a figure of speech, a *kenning*, a poetic device whose name I'd learned in college from my annotated copy of *Beowulf.* Kennings a feature of English poetry before English was exactly English, English when it was young copying the habit of other Germanic languages that combine a couple words or maybe more than a couple words into one; a compounded, omnibus, agglutinated, portmanteau word whose meaning does not simply combine the meanings of words it conjoins but creates a new, different word, one that both retains the particular meaning of familiar words forming it, but also, just as the convention of marriage transforms each partner, a kenning changes the meaning of words which constitute it. When you see words linked together for the first time as a kenning (sometimes dashes serve as chains to connect a kenning's coffle of words, sometimes not), it's like seeing newlyweds for the first time the morning after they have taken their vows. You look and look again, guess and guess again, wondering who these people you thought you knew have become. Who they might be. Might have been. Will be.

Sheppard can consult no database to learn how many Africans have been kidnapped. No database has been organized, nor even conceived at the end of the nineteenth century. Plenty of counting going on always, but counting and accounting to keep track of profit, not of individual lives. William Henry Sheppard crosses the Atlantic during April of 1899, thus he can only guess how many Africans have been killed, captured, enslaved. How many imprisoned in fortified holding pens commanded by Europeans where captive Africans were bought and sold, then transported in shiploads to foreign continents and islands where they were bought and sold again. Merchandise like butchered animal carcasses or pots and pans.

Impossible for Sheppard or anyone else to number exactly the victims. Any number as unverifiable as the amount of suffering an

African—child, woman, man—endured crossing this whale-road, this flesh railroad, and no contemporary database, no matter how sophisticated, can render today an inkling of that quantity, that quality of suffering either. So why bother to count. What do the numbers mean anyway, Sheppard might ask or guess or wonder or sigh or weep or moan. Better to imagine himself as poet, entitle himself to interrogate himself like those Olde English bards or Old Norse bards, with their kennings when they gazed at cold, endless expanses of sea, at the uselessness of all words they had learned to describe their sensations, their experience of gut, fingers, toes as they drown and disappear each time they confront the enigma, the infinity of an ocean's icebound, unfathomable heart which certainly, after all, was not a heart at all, not any word known, so if you attempt to write the truth of it, best to pretend as poets pretend when they say they write from the heart, though poets understand very well that the heart they say is responsible for words they write is certainly not the warm organ inside them pumping blood through the body, not that heart any more than that piece-of-meat heart is what Sheppard searches for as he stares and stares over the ship's railing at a cold, heartless sea, staring and looking for words as poets do when they write poems, on some good days anyway, when all things seem possible, and he attempts to invent a different word, another word, not heart, not mind, not exactly gut, toes, fingers clinging, not alive or dead, a kenning rather, a figure of speech, a *slaveroad* consisting of body after African body, and though he cannot say how many, surely more than enough enslaved bodies, one after another, laid head to foot, foot to head, to create a *slaveroad* crossing the Atlantic Ocean, reaching from Africa to this New World.

African bodies and some like his, mixed like him, William Henry Sheppard thinks, not exactly only African bodies, he's sure, but sure all the bodies on the slaveroad are people's bodies and you can try to count them for yourself if you disbelieve him, doubt his numbers, his count, count them yourself, one by one, stepping on them, in them if you dare, as I must dare and S must dare, to count them, touch them, no choice, the only accurate accounting must be step by step, body by body, bodying our way across the wide, cold Atlantic on a *slaveroad* that brought us here, all those bodies not alive, not dead either, but stretching across the sea. Bodies enough and more Sheppard guesses to form a multilane slaveroad all the way from one world to another, a slaveroad crossing oceans, bodies floating substantial atop the water, and he can go back and forth forever, on not a phantom highway but a slaveroad, persisting, timeless as time, never floating away, and every now and then traffic so thick, so sticky and stinky and sloppy underfoot you slip and slide and wince and cry out and groan as you watch others crossing, each one in a separate lane, glimmering or deeply shadowed lanes imagined so each body does not sink and vanish, a lane offering guidance, hope perhaps, that other bodies are alive or dead, coming or going to support your crossing.

And though you remain you, you and only you, you are also somebody so much like you that you can't always tell the difference on this slaveroad. Captives bear captives within themselves. No one's free. Doesn't make a difference, coming or going, dead or alive, on this slaveroad afloat upon a whale-road that bears your weight, Sheppard's weight, weight of others, the weight of feet, pain, clinging fingers, guts. On this slaveroad, the weight is yours, not maybe or maybe not, but certainly, absolutely, you are both you and the others, they are you, who you are, as always, and of course, they remain also who they are, and are you, me, each one of us a distinct word then another word, and more, more words, but also captives of a single unfathomable word *slave*, a body borne on a slaveroad, the kenning announces, and that kenning may help you dream you are alive, dream a new person, perhaps, if you can bear to say the word, go there, say the kenning, say it to yourself, or write it, step after step, body after body, from here to there, there to here. *Slaveroad* a new, different word, not an empty word like those I hear invented, repeated by voices mocking mine while I struggle, splash, spatter, crushing bones and meat, crossing a slaveroad, so many bodies, so much death underfoot to cross this cold sea. Captives of captives inside ourselves we are afraid to let go.

Appalled-abused-ashamed-unforgiving-maimed-guilty-lost-found. A second kenning I might construct. Another poetic device. Poetic license. How I got over, how I got over.

Sheppard stares. I stare. What do we see: Deeep blue sea / Veree deeep blue sea / Willyboy got drownded in the deeep blue sea. Women's voices carry him away as he listens, carry him away on his stare. He wishes he could listen forever to the women singing, forever he wishes and understands or remembers as I do, and wants to listen forever to the women sing, or listen however much longer than forever it takes their lamentation to bring Willyboy home, however long or deep the voices must plunge, must sing before a lost son, their golden boy, returns, standing tall, walking on water, dancing on air as if he's never forgotten those tricks.

Dead so long. Writing Sheppard is a kind of listening. A kind of resignation. Each word a lamentation. Each word erases him to remember him.

But I promised a story. So I will write Sheppard's story. Stop wasting my time, a reader's patience and time. Wasting words doomed to float and sink on this slaveroad.

Who is William Henry Sheppard. What does he see when he's staring at the sea. Who is he to me. Who am I to him. Who am I. What is an autobiography? An Otto biography?

The edges of Manhattan Island sink into the sea. If I walk to an edge and hover there now, and stare down, do I see what Sheppard sees.

Some days the women's singing reaches you, plunges you beyond cold, beyond time, far, far deeper than most moments dangle you. So much city around you. Above. Below. How tall is it. How much does it weigh. How many hearts beating in a vast city surrounding you. A city that sinks fast, turning to nothing faster than you do as you listen and plunge faster than the slaveroad brings you here, brings the missionary William Henry Sheppard here to live and die and cross and recross the sea on missions to England to Kentucky to Congo to Virginia to Kuba Kingdom. Sheppard tells his story to you in an instant while you stand beside him and listen. Stare with him at cities, lives, ghosts drowned thirty or forty feet below your eyes, below your hands gripping a steel railing, down there inches away where cold sea licks at the edge of Domino Park in Brooklyn, at the Lower East Side edge of New York City.

Reality is the stuff I am made of and what I make of that stuff. Snips and snails and puppy dog tails. Or sugar and spice and all things nice. What do you think. Who are you. One or the other. Are you a little boy or little girl. Or colored girl or colored boy. Different and colored and separate according to whose decision, whose decree, whose words. When the ship docks, whose singsong, doggerel voice separates captain, crew, passengers from cargo. Snips and snails from sugar and spice. A nursery rhyme Sheppard may have heard in his century as I hear it chanted in mine. And which century, which city is this one I see now, these towers, bridges, tunnels, steeples, bodies sinking, rising from the cold, cold sea.

Born in one century, Sheppard dies in another. A fate I will share. Does he feel more at home in the century of his birth, then more like a stranger in his second century, after home, mother and father long gone. Him growing older, passing through time or time passing through him, inevitable transition, an almost effortless effort, daily business consuming him, vexing him, ordinary, casual, tedious business often, but mysterious beyond words as he tries to recall how it felt to leave behind one century, leave it and in an instant discover it's lost and long ago. Him working to envision a second century looming on the horizon, time here, solid, solid, feeling it here, there, solid, just beyond what's visible as Sheppard stands on a ship's deck staring, centuries invisible, one century passed then another century passing, another on its way because someone has decreed it, and decreed that he surely will not reach the next century on its way, not stretch, not endure, not go to wherever, whatever's there. Him still ignorant as a stone about time though he's had two chances, life in two separate centuries to figure time out.

And should I concede that neither Sheppard nor I will ever figure it out. Helpless as words, as songs, as poems and novels.

Time does not pass. Time does not speak. Sheppard does not speak. He stares and listens. Voices of the singing women subside. Nothing. Willyboy does not stride nor boogey from the sea. Wrong place, wrong century.

Though on this slaveroad we are still enslaved, we are not slaves. Not me, not Sheppard, not Willy, the lost golden boy. Not Rebekah, your fellow missionary, she's not a slave either, Sheppard. Rebekah a woman who traveled the slaveroad before you, Sheppard. Rebekah whose voice blends into the women's singing that I wish some days I could listen to forever. None of us slaves. Each separate, each a very different person, one from the other, and the same person, too, though divided, too, each of us bearing many inside the one we happen to be at any given moment during this mysterious passage of time we're allotted, our time and not ours, each of us a person encompassed inside by time's silence, silence separate from whatever else we may be, the many, many voices always clamoring, singing always inside us that nobody else ever hears, except when we become them a moment, become one of the others we always are, the many voices speaking inside us, inside me. And each voice suddenly as lonely as I am when I am stricken by inconsolable aloneness and find myself asking, *Is Sheppard here. Is Rebekah here.* Ask because aren't all of us always here, always different perhaps, always perhaps the same here, here on this slaveroad though each of us no one's slave.

Have you heard her, Sheppard. Heard Rebekah's voice singing in the chorus of women calling Willyboy home, Rebekah's voice despite the fact some other facts would allege that R sailed across the Atlantic long before you were conceived, let alone born, Sheppard. Rebekah alive on the Caribbean island of St. Thomas, then crossing the ocean first time to Europe, west to east, same direction of your first Atlantic crossing to Africa, S, and years later she crosses it again, returns as you do, Sheppard, back to Africa, but she dies there and you are still not born.

Perhaps that's where and when I should begin this autobiography. My missionary story. Not with you, Sheppard, but her. With Rebekah crisscrossing the slaveroad from the Caribbean islands to Europe, then back to Africa, and deciding to die in Africa, but never an end to her mission because, in a manner of speaking, it never ends for anybody—not for Rebekah, nor you, Sheppard, nor me. Those precarious crossings and recrossings, enslaved but never slaves, though dedication to a mission, a god, an art, a person, an idea, or simply dedication to the choice to survive, may unavoidably enslave us all, perhaps.

I stare, listen, study, bear witness to witnesses surrounding me who bear witness here and there on this slaveroad, this miry clay, this long, long road of bloody flesh, this unthinkable, unsinkable confusion that buoys and drowns me, my breath and bleeding thereupon.

Help me, Jesus: my mom's better way of expressing all of the above.

WHO IS REBEKAH

Who is this Rebekah, Sheppard asks. Or rather, I have him ask in order to tell this story. His, mine, hers. This story of a slaveroad that sustains us to this day and time where we find ourselves. Or rather seek ourselves. Mourning our dead. Our deaths.

Allow this story to offer itself as if it's news. As if reading it might be beneficial, as if the story's source exists somewhere other than inside of me. As if the words also are another's story, as if readers may discover themselves in this story and, if not exactly saved by it, are distracted by it from whomever they usually are or are not.

Rebekah Protten is buried, I believe, not far from the walls of Fort Christiansborg (aka the Castle), located near the Ghanaian city of Osu, north and east of your old Congo stomping grounds, Sheppard. Fort Christiansborg, citadel and castle, erected in the 1660s and prospering for centuries as a major holding pen and depot where captive African people were bought and sold. In 1902 Fort C became the seat of contemporary Ghana's government, an obvious irony, given the site's appalling past. Now Fort C serves mainly as a tourist attraction.

Once upon a time, back when Alex Haley's *Roots* started to inspire many people to investigate their African descent, my very smart, lucky, firstborn son earned a fellowship that bought him a ride on the slaveroad and enabled him to cross the Atlantic, leave America, and study for a year in Ghana at an institute named in honor of W.E.B. Du Bois. You, Sheppard, like me, most likely too busy, too ensconced in your missionary duties to find time to visit, let alone learn the history of an old Danish fort in present-day Ghana. Were you as ignorant as I was of Fort Christiansborg's centuries-old role as a hub in the African slave trade's horrific commerce in human bodies. Ignorant of the extraordinary, chaotic careers of an African man, Philip Quaque, and two men of mixed African and European descent—Christian Jacob Protten, Rebekah's husband, and Jacobus Elisa Johannes Capitein—who served as pastors and chaplains in a string of slaving forts along Ghana's southern coast. Perhaps both of us unaware of Christiansborg's intimate presence in our lives, and I remained ignorant until my son returned home from Ghana and began to educate me. You and I, equally in the dark, S, until just yesterday, until this writing and reading I need to share with you about me, about a slaveroad, about Rebekah, her possible grave beneath the stone walls of an ancient fortified city.

A minor miracle, it seems to me—and maybe not so minor the more I contemplate the wonder of it—that Rebekah discovered ways to ignore the decrees of harbormasters in St. Thomas or London or Nantes or Amsterdam or Accra or Madrid or Lisbon, the absolute decrees intended to separate absolutely and forever passengers from cargo. Decrees, I believe, mattering little to R, despite the often deadly consequences such decrees could entail. Whether or not she was abused, treated as chattel, as somebody's property from the very first moments of her life, R must have understood somehow that freedom is the most primal, most profound and fatal separation. And thus the presence of other forms of separation and segregation decreed by her captors could not intimidate nor control R. Words spoken or written or enforced by others would not alter the image of herself she bore. Decrees of foreigners might doom African lives, doom their color, but did not define Africans. Another voice ruled, she was certain. Nameless, colorless, unbound by place and time, powerful beyond words any language could invent. A voice for R that presided within the vast, swirling darkness that rules oceans, fire, sun, moon, stars. Voice freeing her. Voice compounded of mysterious imperatives all creatures great and small obey. Voice unreachable by petty decrees of petty tyrants, by laws of mighty empires, by edicts of kings or queens. A voice impervious to all noises humans make, except perhaps the humblest whimper or prayer.

Rebekah, twice widowed, both her children long dead, one dead daughter from each of her dead marriages, and one leg dead now, too, as R totters below Christiansborg's walls. She walks on one whole leg that's left, drags the other limb, a wobble, a lean to keep from falling, a cane to preserve her balance on the leg that still works more or less as it should, the other leg withered, scarred, crooked, a wraith of dead weight that belongs to Rebekah, but only makes its presence known to her as fire burning or numbness cold as the cold sea.

Both legs equal and strong once upon a time, good legs that had carried her tirelessly to every corner of St. Thomas, all hours of the day or night, anywhere on the island she hoped she might find ears willing to listen, to attend a minute, an hour, a day to her words, hear the message it was her sacred mission to carry and share. Her mission despite the fact her words always disappointed her. Failed her. Never quite expressed what she yearned for them to say to other souls. Fumbling words. Faltering, inadequate words. Words shaming her.

But she would press on. Again and again. Failing or not failing, she would not concede. On a mission. Determined to speak to others the message, the words of the voice that burned inside her, though her heart understood she was unworthy, an impure vessel for carrying and rendering the voice driving her to spread its truth. Truth of the soul within her, truth the voice had revealed to her, truth lifting her, freeing her when unexpectedly, every now and then, her poor, plain words stirred a shout, a grunt, or when a line of scripture she recites is murmured, repeated louder, then a chorus of murmuring, almost a song from souls gathered round her in the darkness, truth propelling her from one end to the other of the green island of St. Thomas, farm to farm, plantation to plantation, hovel to hovel, on paths through forests, alongside cultivated fields, beside streams; streams a trickle in one season, then rushing torrents, changeable as the ground under her feet as earth rises, falls, carved, furrowed to climb hills or circle round them, familiar contours of the land rising visible against the horizon, or spreading before her in unfathomably gentle waves like the sea when it's calm.

Not like the murderous surf constantly pounding Fort Christiansborg's walls, but restful, murmuring blue-green sea that usually surrounds St. Thomas, the island she recalls that once surrounded her, a bright island her eyes could see plainly in daylight, then at night must recall and negotiate because she could not depend upon sight, only upon blindness, memory, guesses, the steadiness of her breath, her heart, their regular drumbeats her only company in utter darkness. Yet better than no company at all, she'd work to remind herself. Her body, the small squinting life inside her thumping away always, yet as meager, as feeble as that creature's presence might feel, wasn't it always there, surprising, freeing her some moments like thin moonlight that would occasionally open a way on the darkest night.

Most treks on St. Thomas undertaken alone, in darkness, as they must be, in order to avoid being observed by dangerous eyes as she pursues her mission, pursuing enslaved souls in the dead of night because she must. At night because other people's eyes are more dangerous than eyes of hungry, prowling beasts, beast eyes scouring the dark for prey, and she relies on night to hide her from human eyes, depends on her silence, depends on her relentless strides, scrambles, stumbles, narrow escapes from falling or drowning to make her way from plantation to plantation, through vast darkness deepened by anonymous insect twittering, by sudden swooping birds, shrieks, an enormous, unpredictable dark swollen by unnamable threats, a terrifying silence containing worse terrors than anything a person able to hear or imagine.

But that vast silence is tame compared to a silence she felt once, draining and entrapping her, vast silence Rebekah might try to explain by telling a story to the two of us, to William Henry Sheppard and myself, story about silence engulfing a room she was cleaning in the baronial mansion of Master Boehm, a gentle patron of African suffering, Boehm who welcomed on his plantation the Moravian Brethren and Sisters and permitted a few local, unenslaved womenfolk of color, like me, Rebekah says, to assist the Moravians in their efforts to awaken and salvage souls of the island's enslaved population, create a community of African Christians on St. Thomas. A community including, strange as it may seem, those who inhabited Boehm's immense holdings. He allowed us to preach to his African laborers and servants, some bound to him for a term, others bound forever. Preach also to gangs of Africans passing through, residing on St. Thomas temporarily as workers on Boehm's land and other plantations, Africans destined sooner or later to board again the trade's evil, scavenging ships and disappear from St. Thomas, dying or born again in saltwater oblivion.

A stunning, deadly kind of silence it was, gentlemen, the silence in a room of Master Boehm's mansion that assaulted me one awful day. Silence stifling, devouring me. No space for me, my breath, my heart, though my body captive in a room occupied by Master Boehm's large, large Dutch wife, Mistress Boehm.

Only two of us in the room. Mistress B knitting. Me busy with broom and mop and bucket and rags at a task it was my duty to accomplish, scrubbing the parlor floor until its oak planks gleamed bright as a polished apple's skin, but on that hateful afternoon, I felt a dizzying instant of utter weakness and exhaustion and it forced me to pause in my labors, attempt to address a few apologetic words to Mistress Boehm, words that I hoped might excuse my slowness, my need to pause, explain my distress. Words to which the response of Mistress Boehm was utter silence and a hesitation growing palpably more ominous to me the longer she chose not to speak. I feared that she'd begun to savor the silence she had initiated. That she wanted silence in the room to thicken, expand.

Finally her eyes slowly rose up from her knitting and fixed upon my face an unblinking stare. Her voice broke the silence. Her imperial, haughty, impervious, omnivorous voice drowning me, swallowing the world.

In her story as she relates it to us, Rebekah recalls Mistress Boehm's words as a deluge, a flood, but now I think I would translate R's words for *flood* and *deluge*—as *slaveroad*, if ever I transcribed them, because slaveroad is what I have come to understand R was describing, and I wonder what word or words, if any, Sheppard might have turned over in his mind while he listened to R say she was drowning in a *flood* . . . a *deluge*.

Sheppard, like me, grappling to grasp what R's words mean. Though I must be honest here and admit that neither Sheppard's American ears nor mine are able to compute reliably what the good, dignified, long-suffering old biddy Rebekah strives to communicate in her highly accented, idiosyncratic English, her polyglot of pidgins riddled with Danish, Fanti, Dutch, Ga, German, Akan, etc., producing in us amazement, curiosity, a yearning to decipher, but at best, only intermittent moments of comprehension. Bursts, flashes, intimations as we work to imagine what it might be R had experienced and is endeavoring to relate.

Silence, evil and enormous silence, filling the parlor, good sirs, until large Mistress Boehm's large icy voice crashes it, trashes it as she mocks my voice, mocking me precisely as she accuses me of mocking her.

Upon your leave, you say. You dare say that to me. *Upon your leave, Mistress*, you say. How dare you, girl. How dare you steal my words, echo my speech, you pitiful parrot.

Upon your leave, you say. Upon your leave, oh blessed Mistress and kindest of benefactors. I am quite, quite weary, you say, and say, upon your leave, Mistress, may I rest, please, please, I must rest a moment, please, you say. Words spoken truly in a ladylike fashion, or rather the ragtag fashion of the lady you fancy yourself to be, day after day since arriving here destitute, starving at our back gate, begging alms or bread or a day's work. You, abandoned, discarded there, an orphan, I hasten to remind you, not the lady you presume you are.

You forever presuming yourself to be far better than you are, wench. You presuming that our charity to you is matched or overmatched by the charity you extend to us by your decision to stay and serve us. Sharing yourself, displaying yourself as you imitate a lady, the lady you will never be, girl, though you curtsy and bow and slut yourself around here in my parlor when in fact I have granted you no such *leave*, neither to pause in your chores nor to address me as your equal. No leave, certainly, to sass and disobey, you presumptuous little bitch.

In which of my armchairs, by your leave, do you wish to sit and rest your delicate self, dear fatigued lady. Do you dare imply we share common ground. Dare to suggest that monthly pangs which do not spare even the noblest born of ladies are irresistibly sapping your strength today. That the seeping of your impure blood licenses you to do as you please. To defy me.

By your leave, please, Madame, I must abandon a few moments the labors that you require me to perform. Tasks imposing suffering beyond endurance. That's what you believe, isn't it, and thus you demand a bit of a rest before completing your duties. Oh, you poor, dear, tender, frail, imposed-upon, unfortunate, darling, ladylike thing.

After her menacing silence, Mistress Boehm's booming, menacing voice floods the parlor, drowning me. Her words twist my words, as her voice skewers me, rattles on and on, resonating, crackling with mirthless laughter, shouts, giggles, until she stops. Then a second silence reigns, silence following her flood of words, absolute, seething silence she dared me to disturb, to enter, to challenge with even a single, solitary syllable. Silence like the mouth of a cannon loaded, primed, and aimed at my face. Silence prepared to thunder louder than her booming voice. Silence ready to blow out my brains if I spoke or not, spoke too soon or too late.

Silence reigns again until Mistress B grunts up from the chair consecrated as her knitting station and crosses the parlor, crosses much more quickly than I ever recalled having seen her move her bulk, darting from overstuffed armchair to fireplace, where she snatches up a poker leaned against heated stones, a mistake bringing a sudden yelp, a furious wringing of the naked hand that had touched warm iron, but undeterred, she swiftly, carefully, cursing like a trooper, grabs whatever she was knitting and wraps it round the poker so that she can grasp it comfortably in both fists to strike me, one, two . . . a third excruciating blow before I drop to the floor and receive the balance of blows and afterthought stomps from which I have never recovered.

My injuries treated by a ship's doctor, a guest boarding in the Boehm mansion drinking himself nightly into a stupor courtesy of Master Boehm's liquor. A surgeon he claimed himself to be, and kindly, generously demanding no fee, he cut into me, attempted to repair and refigure my bones, sewed me up while I was delirious, unconscious, fevered.

He bled me, I recall, once I had awakened, a necessary, salubrious cleansing, he insisted, though it very nearly drained the final dregs of my vital spirits. Drunk, puffed up, as if his skills had succeeded in keeping me alive, the good doctor blessed me the morning of the day he boarded the *Alexander*, the ship he served that had been languishing in calm waters offshore far too long while its captain was ashore, the captain slowly then frantically negotiating to sell and buy cargo, turn that handsome profit the owners always expected. But an unpredictable scarcity of African bodies in St. Thomas's dungeon, a shortage that the best of captains would occasionally encounter and could not remedy, no matter his negotiating skills, no matter how adroitly he could turn to his advantage exchanges of merchandise for bodies, bodies for merchandise. Without an ample, available supply of Africans in the dungeon, any captain would disappoint a ship's owners, and thus the *Alexander*, a disappointed ship when it finally departed, then was lost at sea along with my good doctor and all other souls aboard. The *Alexander* never completing the triangular voyage home, missing a leg, like me now, kind sirs, though I survived Mistress Boehm's assault. She did not deliver a fatal blow, but left me to hobble around on one decent leg, the other maimed, slowly rotting inside.

I survived like many others who survived or evaded, or weathered horrors administered by men and women whom the trade elevated to godlike status, bestowing upon them fabulous riches and impunity. But that prosperous commerce that killed many and nearly killed me could also kill its perpetrators, drown them on the slaveroad as it drowned the *Alexander*'s captain, crew, their cargo of Africans.

Good, feeble Master Boehm trumpeted his outrage at his evil wife's treatment of me, though only privately to her, never forcing her to acknowledge publicly the sin of grievous abuse of me, though she was compelled to pretend to nurse and pamper me a whole month before she resumed her customary goading and plaguing, tormenting me until the day she died. She lived long enough to witness my increasingly limping gait, the invisible destruction and deterioration going on inside my shattered limb. Years passed and never once an expression of regret, let alone apology.

My damaged leg grew worse and worse till this very instant of my old age as I stand here or, rather more truthful to say, totter here, beside an ancient African fort's whitewashed walls, a ghost quietly whispering to warn you about a sort of crocodile concealed within a dark river of silence, a beast whose jaws, faster than an eye blinks, will yawn open, snap shut, and impale you on long, yellow teeth.

I was—am—a casualty, and I hover still at the margins, Rebekah announced to us. Dependent, despairing, waiting, searching, praying for the voice inside me to return and break awful silences one after another. To help me escape oppressive, everlasting, enforced silence of being the woman I am. Voice to lead, guide, reassure me. As words in the sacred book, the sacred songs promised. Voice instructing me how to share its power. To speak its bright truth to darkened minds, to hearts ignorant of the soul's presence.

Soul present and eternal within even the most benighted ones, R believes. Gift of a precious soul residing in all bodies. Soul there, unalterably there. Born there and a body needs only to listen to its own beating, fleshy heart to hear the soul's summons. A voice offering salvation, life everlasting. Voice there forever beside her, within her, beside, within all of us. Within naysayers, yea-sayers, those aware or unaware of the precious soul they bear, R said. Soul speaking or chorus of souls singing finally on the day the finders and keepers of soul transported to the blessed kingdom, a peaceful realm, far, far distant from cruel islands of toil and misery and torture and death dooming captive Africans.

Cruel islands like that green St. Thomas she had roamed in her youth. Roaming, restless, undeterrable. Not reckless, yet determined to pursue her soul's mission wherever that pursuit led. Or cost. Pursuing her mission on two legs, one leg, none, to deliver wherever, whenever she's able, the good news of a gift humankind bears, good news of an immortal soul which if embraced, frees a person. Even one lost, poor, and destitute as she was, is. Even one crippled. One decreed cargo and colored and separate as once and apparently forever she had been condemned to be.

And now in these last days, by refusing to cross the slaveroad again (the Moravians offered to pay her return passage from Africa back to the Americas), she truly is, R believes, by her own decree, an African again. Not desperate to exchange one world for another. Not free to erase the miserable, sinful, desperate, thrashing, cruel existence she has suffered. But grants herself in her old age the power to choose a sort of niggling, trifling peace beside Christiansborg's walls.

Is R curious about the two men who pay her a visit. Do they truly wish to hear her speak. Did they arrive on human feet. Or is she dreaming them, a dream she can't exactly recall or fears or chooses not to recall. Wary. Wariness causing her to hesitate, as she had hesitated long ago, to enter the trap of silence, trap of futile confrontation that loud, large Mistress Boehm had constructed, spilled, spewed in her parlor like cheese to silently lure a mouse.

These men with their odd language, their skin not dark African brown but whited brown like hers. Where do they come from. Do they possess homes, families, villages, nations. Or are both of them wanderers like her. Wanderers, spirits uprooted, misplaced, displaced. Missionaries seeking souls of others. And their own.

Should she tell them or not, her visitors, these two who seem strangers, foreigners at times, at other times familiar kin, tell them about her shame. Should she reveal to them, speak to them in any fashion, about the special ministrations Master B began upon her in his mansion as she lay immobile, recuperating, two centuries and a half ago, from Mistress B's savage beating.

Why had she kept silent when Master Boehm's ministrations commenced. Why silence then or now. Who, what prevents her speaking out, crying out. Complicity. Shame, fear, pride, loyalty.

Loyalty to whom. Fear of whom. Ashamed of whom. Whose pride. A complicity with whom. With what. Whose disgrace, another's or her own would she be exposing. Whose pride defended by silence. Offended by silence. What would the consequences be, if she confessed.

Confessed? A confession of what, to whom.

Nobody's business, she concludes. Keep your silence, she concludes, promising herself she will. Besides, she concludes—anyway, she concludes—who listens. What would be the point of telling anyone. Who would profit. Whose life saved, destroyed.

Would long-dead Master and Mistress B hear her speak. Does her old, sore, crippled body, itself so near to death, wish to hear sorrowful, pained reminisces of outrages committed upon it.

No. Keep her silence. Impenetrable silence preserved like silence of closemouthed African men in the stories Akan and Fanti people tell here, tell about Africans who man long canoes, African canoes essential to the trade as supplies of African bodies—children, men, women, corpses—imprisoned in Fort Christiansborg's underground warehouse. African arms paddling long canoes loaded with cargo, with bodies back and forth between shore and full-masted, ocean-going vessels anchored safely beyond crashing surf that barricades this coast of what one day will be called Ghana, a barrier that surely would mangle and crush any large sailing vessel's foolhardy effort to breach the white-capped tumult of breakers, the hull-splintering, massive black stones concealed beneath the waves, waves into which oars are driven by African arms, rippled arms the stories say are god-blessed, sun- and sweat-darkened, salt-water-wet arms powerful enough to hold a canoe steady when a wave stands it and its cargo perpendicular to the water, or keep paddling when a canoe is dragged under or chased by a white-hooded, furling wave inches behind, rushing to catch, overtop, and drench it, drown it, swallow it, but fabled African arms rooting, digging into the sea, arms schooled since boyhood to slice straight and on course despite currents pulling, swirling simultaneously in every direction at once, silent arms though the rowers holler, squeal, curse, halloo, laugh, gasp, sing to, and challenge and mock the battering waves, mock themselves, as if they are playing games and not risking life and limb struggling back and forth from shore to placid water out where big ships moored.

African rowers surviving and telling no tales of the business, the commerce, the prospering, consuming trade they make possible and sustain, the body- and soul-consuming terror, remorse, peril, murder, the ferrying back and forth in long canoes, over and over, to feed their families and themselves, feed all the towns and outposts along the coast, you could say, but the rowers wouldn't say, don't say, do not tell tales, do not brag or lament or reminisce about the commands they follow, games they play, chances they take. The rowers maintain a strict silence in the midst of people they don't know, people they have no reason to trust, though perhaps sometimes among themselves, each within himself or aloud in a crowd of other African oarsmen on land or sea, they would curse the vile, deadly labors they perform. That work they could choose not to do, but what else can they do, what else can she do.

R follows the example of the rowers. Maintains her silence among strangers. Guards her anger. Informs no one of Master B's special ministrations. Waits for the moment that may or may not arrive for her, the moment when she's among others like herself who would understand her silence, who themselves have chosen silence, others who do what they must do silently, until they choose to holler, shout, whisper, weep, scream—STOP . . . STOP . . . STOP. Say, Never again. Stop. Stop.

During an interval, not long after my gracious doctor's ship departed the island, as I lay immobile in a bed in one of the closet-sized, always cruelly overcrowded rooms designated as servants' quarters, but one set aside for me to occupy alone as I convalesced,

Master Boehm began his special ministrations. Later, the stage for his ministrations was his office and study, *library*, is what he called the large wood-paneled room containing desk, sofa, and bed. The library, I suppose, since against one wall a shelf of books. But first, in one of the numerous, tiny rooms that served as barracks for house slaves, one of countless cells you would scowl at as a surfeit of rooms in the immense Boehm mansion if it was your duty to keep them all clean, there, while I was still helplessly confined to a bed, my life dangling by a thread, Master B would slip in silently, slip his hands under the bedcovers, and rub my bare legs. Especially solicitous, I could discern, of the injured one, but rubbing, massaging both, the leg battered by Mistress Boehm and the sound leg he would praise a year or so later by exclaiming, My, my, the good Lord endowed you with a perfect, perfect limb, sweet girl, and your other limb soon will be as perfect again.

Master Boehm a proud man. Shy and proud. Proud of his great wealth, his vast holdings immaculately maintained, his leadership in the community of St. Thomas landowners, his role as confidant and adviser to governors sent to the island by the Danish Crown to command the soldiers and superintend trade and traffic in the port. Proud to be an Elder in the Presbyterian Church. Proud, too, perhaps, of his large wife, her astute management of their social responsibilities, her skill as relentless, sparkling, acid conversationalist, dependable hostess, tireless gatherer and purveyor of island gossip. Perhaps also angered and ashamed by his wife's worse than brutal attack on me. Grateful perhaps to me for not publicly announcing her treatment of me, grateful for the fact that I never proclaimed aloud to him his wife's guilt. Pleased further by my willingness to confirm to those who asked about my mishap, a tale, a rumor—admit my disastrous tumble from a tall ladder in a Boehm orchard occurred in pursuit of fruit, my reckless, childish, unauthorized pursuit of apples probably not ripe yet, though gilded by sunlight decorating a tree's highest branches.

Of Master B's initial special ministrations upon me while I lay in a semiconscious, somnolent state, I have only vague recollections. A not excessively unpleasant experience of muted surprise almost, that any sensations other than constant, racking pain—any sensations dim and fugitive as they might be—could be aroused within my battered flesh, within my shattered awareness of a person named R who I might be, or used to be, or could perhaps become once again if I prayed hard and the Great God willing.

I did not flinch from, nor resent, nor resist Master B's touch once I started to fully realize the hands stroking, caressing my bare skin were his. Did not attribute evil motives to him as he commenced his special ministrations. No more than I had attributed pride and vanity as the sole motivations for his efforts to be a pillar of success in St. Thomas society. His attempts to prove here, and also to the European world with which the trade connected the island, that exemplary lives were possible in these colonies.

Silent, infrequent, special ministrations of short duration until I was back on both feet again. Then continuing, but infrequent. Once, twice, three times in a month at most, lasting never more than minutes, sporadic sessions, unpredictable, driven by impulse, I suppose, but continuing until the large presence of Mistress B gone forever, and no hiding, no concealment, no moderation absolutely necessary. Even then, however, the special ministrations no more frequent, nor any longer than in the past, except they became intrusions upon my person I could not endure.

Remove your clothes please, sweet child. Smock, dress, rags, gown, flour-sack, please, girl. Lie upon your belly or back, love, whichever you choose, my friend. And so I did. Sometimes under a covering, sometimes not, depending upon Master Boehm's mood or whim or weather, sessions starting with naked me under his bare hands beneath a blanket perhaps, with strokes probably not intended to be caresses, but respectful, dutiful, quiet, lingering strokes, though suddenly, during some sessions, a blanket, cold day or hot, would be snatched off, tossed aside, the rubbing, prodding, probing harder, faster before it subsided again to a ritualized, rhythmic piety. A sad, quiet intensity resumed, with or without him releasing one of those small furtive moans he probably believed he could conceal from me or maybe it gave him pleasure to imagine I might overhear those small, rare moans I grew to hate, detest, almost as much as I hated the one small moan escaping me during years of countless special ministrations, a moan, truly more gasp than moan, escaping my lips when he undid from between my legs the bloody cloth tucked there.

Yes, I must admit Master Boehm's visitations persisted year after year. Further, admit that I did not actively, adamantly resist. In truth, for a long while, perhaps I did not profoundly resent his attentions. We simply shared a secret between us, I assumed. And hurt no one, I assumed.

But before you condemn me, consider yourself surrounded as I was surrounded by wolves. Imagine yourself familiar with one he-wolf who, though possessing an ugly habit of biting and mauling you, that particular wolf seemed to harbor no inclination to devour you. Would you not choose the company of the familiar wolf, *your* wolf, so to speak, rather than risk the embraces of a new, strange wolf or risk life alone within a pack of hungry, ravenous wolves.

I cannot say I ever liked his touch.

I never did try to convince myself I liked his touch. Though I could not help but be aware of the silent intensity of his concentration and devotion. Did Master B sincerely believe that he was performing penance, paying reparations for his wife's unconscionable trespass upon me. Penance, compensation while his fingers kneaded, squeezed, stroked my legs, grasped a haunch tightly with a fist until I winced and instinctively twisted away.

He never asked me to touch him. A relief for me. A form of denial for him, perhaps, a penance he paid perhaps for his own irrepressible, unspeakable urges. You could say, I guess, that for my own reasons, I did not question his motives too closely or not closely enough, or better say, perhaps—perhaps, perhaps, perhaps . . . always *perhaps,* too many, too much perhaps—yes and no—so now I will just say, Yes—far too often I allowed him to slip a hand under the bedclothes or flip a sheet or blanket off the bed or sofa to expose me completely. Allowed him to contemplate, to touch my nakedness with his eyes and his fingers, as well as with his trespassing thoughts.

The shivers, shudders, warmth of his bare hands gliding over my bare neck, shoulders, waist, buttocks, legs, never a pleasant sensation, yet once or twice felt almost like a momentary reprieve, a possibility we might converse silently in a language not spoken well by either of us. An exchange of hovering ghost words, unintelligible words, though we both understood they belonged to a language that was sacred, unforgettable. An old, old language of oaths, vows, pledges of allegiances; of words, phrases familiar somehow, speaking somehow of familiar yearnings we might wish to embody, but knew we never could. No exchange possible. We knew better. While skins touched, our flesh foolish for an instant like Africans pretending to be safe, protected by Fort Christiansborg's whitewashed walls and rows of cannons.

Captive Africans on St. Thomas, and here beneath the fort's ramparts, celebrate their holidays and feasts by telling stories in broken languages, singing half-understood words of ancestors' songs. Songs whose words have lost their meaning, meanings that can never be recovered. Lost like words Master B and I dared not say aloud to each other for fear their ancient cadences and rhythms might preserve or disclose crucial information about ourselves. Our longings, proud aspirations, fears, shyness, regrets, loneliness, outrage, hungers.

Conversations between B and myself silent collisions. Skin to skin. Not seductive. Fatal. Dead. Words missing. Misunderstood.

Old lovers' tales recycled, but only in unsaid words floating back and forth between us; borrowed, faltering, disguised words, *Hi, Hello, Hello again, Bye again, No, Yes, See you soon, No, Never again* . . . pitiful words, pitiless words, words like bodies drowned, bodies inhabited on a slaveroad that carries us to distant islands, to destinations like this infernal, invisible exit/entrance at Fort Christiansborg guarded by stone walls and ominous mouths of cannons, here where flourishing commerce in flesh never ceases, bodies exchanged for merchandise, merchandise for bodies, a thriving, sprawling, busy business, a slaveroad opening and closing, summoning us, bearing us far away, our bodies, our flesh guarded, separated, cowering within our skins, skin that is also an iron-barred cell through which we cannot converse, no matter how much we might desire to talk, to ignore dangers, to escape skin that cages us.

Skin divided from skin by deadly surf. By waves roaring, rubbing, kneading, crashing, screaming. Like the cold, roiling sea that holds preying ships at bay a mile or two off the shore of what one day will become Ghana. And did Rebekah dream that one day waves of fabled African canoes will struggle, surge, skim across a murderous gap. Break iron collars, iron chains of sea, and drive slave ships away forever.

Small, silent shudders, shivers during Boehm's ministrations I recall not as intimacies. As warnings, rather, of an indestructible slaveroad dismantling us, sweeping us away, unless, until I became cold, indestructible as wind, as seas.

Sheppard levels a gaze at me, nods at me. You are not Rebekah, his gaze says, and then his gaze, held for another silent instant or two, demands: Who are you.

Who are *you*, I reply. Reply without breaking the silence between us while my eyes search his eyes.

Did Rebekah believe tales about superhero African oarsmen. Did she require, after all, their example.

In the story she tells us, Master Boehm's ministrations persisted. He trespassed again and again, crossed the slaveroad again and again, touching her hips, legs, her body that's both sleeping and alert under his soft, heavy hands.

Master Boehm a generous man. Generous towards her, undoubtedly. Releasing her from duties in the mansion so she could apprentice herself to the Moravians, assist them in their crusade to ignite souls, establish communities of worshippers among Africans, no matter where upon the island of St. Thomas their captors cached them, settled them, forced them to labor.

Generous towards Moravian brothers and sisters he generously permitted to occupy abandoned cottages that were his property, cultivate a farm on his land, and charged them no rent. His charity, his support for their activities, of course, also benefited me directly, R acknowledges. And wasn't that a sign of Master Boehm's respect and affection. One more sign of his unique, unchallengeable status on St. Thomas. A man viewed by his peers as seriously religious, highly principled, powerful, enviable, admirable. This despite the fact that most of his fellow planters disagreed with Master B's stance towards the Moravian missionaries, and perceived the black-robed clerics as potential troublemakers, as uninvited meddlers who might sow seeds of balkiness, rebellion, confusion into childish brains of African workers.

Not a terrible man, after all. Was he or wasn't he.

Was I terrible, R asks. Why the depth of her silence and shame. Her fear, pride, fury, hate, the very same emotions she imagines rowers feel with every stroke of their paddles ferrying bodies back and forth below Fort Christiansborg's walls and guns. The lucrative, human meat-and-bone-eating trade. Trade the African paddlers bound to by generations of kinship and blood. Bound by the necessity to feed families, feed themselves. A trade unsustainable, impossible without them.

But how do they make peace with violence they abide and help to perpetuate. If she asked today, what would the rowers reply to the pitiful phantom she has become. She's heard the stories many times in Fanti and Ga. Heard Africans bragging, praising powerful arms, celebrating the long canoes, the rowers' skills, their miracles of willpower. But certainly the oarsmen themselves would never shout out loud their indispensability, their complicity, their crimes. Who might be listening. Who would choose to reveal dangerous secrets that both glorified and damned them. Bound them to the slaveroad.

Did she envy the rowers, anyway. Envy Master Boehm.

She was not the property of Master Boehm. Boehm not her master. I do not know if, according to the rules governing St. Thomas, Rebekah born free or not. Whether one or both of her parents enslaved or one or the other or both had earned or been granted the legal rights of an unenslaved person. If so, such transactions must have occurred while R very young, too young to remember. But no doubt she was the offspring of two parents, enslaved or not. Two parents necessary, aren't they. Two parents no matter the kind or status of each. That's the universal rule, isn't it. Even if on St. Thomas certain children could claim only the breast, the blood of one parent.

R raised by kind people. Or at least one kind person during her earliest years. Though she also recalls being raised by others surely unkind, doggedly, spitefully unkind, starved people whose hunger and neglect she shared, a bitter portion she learned to accept without complaint, but better times, too, often with strangers whose names she's forgotten, or were they her parents or a single parent prosperous enough to feed and clothe and shelter her decently, then suddenly nobody, no home, R's alone again, learning to follow orders, learning to be grateful for more orders, even when she knows that performing exactly what she's been ordered to do earns her no reward.

R learning to speak in more than one language and to negotiate in other languages she couldn't speak, teaching herself to dress and behave and keep herself clean in whatever manner others deemed appropriate for her, learning to scrub rooms, tend animals, sew, elementary cooking, care of infants, occasional nearly pleasant exchanges, then a time when good fortune, good luck ended abruptly, far too quickly, and nothing again, nowhere to go, only memories, only wishful thinking and regrets, no roof over her head many nights, sleeping in fields or woods, in barns, barnyards, or hiding in a town under a deserted market stall until dawn, then wandering off again, hoping daylight and decent citizens' eyes will help her fend off or recover from the absolutely vicious ones she encounters, evil ones of all colors, sizes, shapes, nations, islands, tribes, clans. The ones who are ruthless, selfish, untrustworthy as she herself became, until, exhausted, she finds herself one dismal spring morning at the back gate of the high brick wall which encloses Master B's mansion, staring at a ten-foot-tall, iron-barred gate with an African servant stationed beside it who watches her approach, and she would have gratefully welcomed the opportunity to batter down bricks and iron with her bare, filthy head and happily have crawled on her hands and knees to kiss the muddy shoes of the servant on duty, if only he would invite her inside.

No. I never demanded that Master Boehm stop his special ministrations. Never summoned up the will or courage or requisite clarity about what I desired, about who I was, who I wanted to be, and commanded him to cease. I believe I possessed insufficient clarity about my own self-interest. Not enough clarity, certainly, about the distinction between resigned, passive acceptance and the kind of acquiescence that encourages trespass. For too long, I did not muster up enough resolve to act. To overcome the fear of loneliness and failure I was sure I'd face again if I lost my place in Master B's service. Fear of suffering I would endure if I forwarded my self-interest in a direct, enlightened fashion.

Never confronted MB and commanded him never again to abuse me. Nevertheless, stop he did. A permanent halt, not unconnected, perhaps, with a tale I conjured and spun for my so-called master Boehm.

I had become engaged to Matthaus Freundlich, a Moravian brother whose colleagues (especially the Sisters) were my helpmates, teachers, catechists, guides on St. Thomas, and with whom, by then, I shared a religion, a mission to enlighten and save souls. The Moravians had chosen me by unanimous vote to be the spouse of Brother Freundlich and counseled him that he should, indeed, marry me, a union both Brother Freundlich and I approved and anticipated would forward and enhance the mission to which both of us had decided to dedicate our lives. After apprising Master Boehm of my engagement, I asked him if his special attentions over the years had a specific name, a Presbyterian name he could share with me. Told MB I was asking for a name so that I could include it in the precise description I intended to give my intended of the special ministrations MB performed upon me. Explained to MB my hope was that the combination of my detailed description and an exact name MB could supply would serve to identify precisely for my scholarly, soon-to-be lawfully wedded husband, the exact nature of MB's attentions. Hoped that my intended would then inform me if Moravian Christians like Presbyterian Christians engaged in such practices and if, like MB and the Presbyterians, they saw no harm in them.

I venture to say that you must have become a different kind of person by that point in your life, Rebekah. May I inquire who you were then. Who are you now, R.

Why did you choose in the midst of what likely was a low-key, even drab conversation about household chores, an interlude of dull questions, of responses equally dull, to turn what seemed at first an ordinary, uninflected gaze upon MB, looking at him but then letting your eyes drift away, ignoring him as your eyes are drifting, as you drift away from the place where you stand or sit, the room where MB also standing or seated, and then your eyes returning quickly, focus sharply upon MB, and your words demand his attention, words that steal his eyes and direct them to see another person's stare, an imminent stare more than possible and probable, an undeniable stare that MB should have seen coming, and did and didn't, until you speak, then he does see it, does imagine exactly the shocked and dismayed stare your almost spouse would fix upon you after you relate to him your precise description of MB's ministrations performed upon your body, and MB must have imagined the same stare fixed upon him, and realized that very soon, at the first opportunity presenting itself by chance, or in a furious hurry, your intended spouse would fix upon him, upon MB, an actual rattlesome, rattled, and rattling stare, the stare that you created, R, in MB's imagination with your story, R.

A fictive gaze, so to speak, but an image alerting and convincing far beyond make-believe's usual, ordinary, harmless prattle.

Did you, R, imagine the gaze, the stare, as writers imagine things they wish, things they imagine and wish for readers to imagine, things writers hope are coming to life larger than life, better, worse, more, less, more false, more true than life, yet so lively, so unblushingly, intimidatingly real and unreal and unavoidable that they could be or, on the other hand, must be true—untrustworthy, believable, unbelievable, acceptable, unacceptable—crushing and possible/impossible as life itself.

Rebekah an artist then. Turning you, Master Boehm, into a fiction she sees, a person she sees, a person her intended spouse sees. A person everybody sees, MB. And you, you too, MB, see that person in all the eyes seeing you.

Do you holler, B. Do you scream, whisper, shout, weep. Stop. Stop. Stop.

I see Rebekah. And she is magical. She's a magician, Master Boehm. R stops you in your tracks. Now you see her/now you don't, Boehm. Losing her, never touching R again. She's lost on a slaveroad, in a looking glass. Down the rabbit hole. Down the hatch. Door of no return. Where oh where does she go.

SHEPPARD

I asked you above, Sheppard—who are you. Let me share more of what I have learned. Despite your silence when I asked. Despite your silence now, Sheppard.

I was determined—despite unforgiving wear and tear, despite the obvious risk of serious injury that running poses for an old body growing more and more fragile daily—to begin jogging again after a two-year hiatus, and yesterday morning I tried and fell. I commend myself for a *why-not*, never-say-die, enough's-never-enough attitude, but also acknowledge the silliness of an eighty-one-year-old man who, just because he's been extraordinarily lucky and able to depend upon services from his body long past the age most men can, remains ungrateful, arrogant, even flippant—after all, as a young guy didn't I win or come close to the top in every competition I chose or was compelled to enter, and didn't the girls I chased often smile if I caught them, a smile inviting me to come round again. Long, hard walks are satisfying in their way, but don't get me sweaty, heart pumping, and didn't I still look more than okay on the beach in swim trunks, if one forgets about flab creases behind my biceps, the soft, million-wrinkled slack skin creeping out from where it sleeps beneath my armpits, spoiling upper edges of still taut slabs of chest. So why the hell not, greedy me insists, still full of myself, insisting upon more, more . . .

Unlike a tumble from an outcropping of huge rocks at the edge of the sea a dozen years or so ago in Brittany, a misstep that led me to acquire a pacemaker, yesterday's fall while jogging was closer to comic than catastrophic. Fortunately, my hands hit the ground first yesterday, and absorbed most of the impact of my airborne weight hurtling forward after I tripped. Every arthritic bone inside my hands receiving a kind of sudden numbing shock, yet, luckily, no bones broken, just one thumb slightly crooked, swelling immediately, and many small scratches, cuts, nicks, and a couple bloody punctures, worst one in my chest, skin everywhere perforated by pebbles, stones, fallen branches, prickly foliage cluttering the floor of a narrow dirt trail I'd chosen to negotiate first day back jogging, trail alongside one of whose edges I land on my belly, lying there surprised, speechless, afraid to move.

Bordered by immense tree trunks and thick undergrowth from which dangled streamers of vines festooned with tiny, needle-sharp spikes, the dirt trail through the woods I'd picked for a jog turned occasionally into a sort of twisting, luminous tunnel, an aisle between steep green and black sides, roofed by overhanging branches. Trail and woods idyllic, serene. Absolutely quiet yesterday, except for my footfalls muffled by piles of leaves that had dropped prematurely during an extended drought, more months of little or no rain than anyone around here could ever recall, grass brown, crops parched, leaves dying, colorful flowers and shrubbery in the middle of July turning autumn dull and rusty everywhere in Brittany, a sure enough sign the internet weather channel announced, of climate change, change some people lamented as fatal already, and more people starting to worry.

Jogging again—even slowly, even though it felt like being suddenly born again in a primeval forest—remained a shaky idea for reasons I've noted, but jogging seduced me, an especially fine choice, a welcome respite from rumors the world about to end in a minute.

Until one side of my face slammed into dirt, roots, stones, gravel, and whatever other miscellaneous, malicious debris hidden by leaves littering the ground upon which I'd landed, stunned, stretched out flat on my belly, curious how long it would take me to stand up, turn around, and get myself back home. Cuts on my cheek, forehead, both lips bleeding, upper lip fat as two or three lips grotesquely crowding my nose by the time I study my face twenty minutes later in a mirror. Wish you and Rebekah could have seen me, Sheppard. My clown face giving you a good laugh. Owe you both a laugh or two, don't I, given my high-handed, one-sided manner of exploiting your stories in order to make sense of mine.

I'm beginning to know Rebekah as well as I know you, Sheppard. Which is, of course, not very well in either case. Though I've written extensively about you and to you before, S. Long before I encountered R on this oddly fluid, transforming, yet eternally fixed slaveroad we all occupy, I had informed myself as best I could about you, read your autobiography, *Presbyterian Pioneers in Congo*, and several books about you, including a recent novel based upon your life. Consumed scholarly essays, newspaper and journal articles. Consulted archives of your photos and personal memorabilia. Studied an illustrated catalog of your gift of African artifacts to a university museum. Results of that formal and informal research are scattered in my fiction and nonfiction of the last several years, and I alert you in advance to expect to see—in whatever this piece of writing turns out to be—words, phrases, passages, information, or scenes I have previously published, and hope their presence will not offend or put to sleep or bore you nor the few faithful followers of my work who may been exposed before, and thus might recognize some of what they find here.

I'm not alerting you, S, because I feel the need to excuse or apologize for repetition. Though I should admit that vanity encourages my probably futile desire to offer readers who have missed and remain happily unaware of anything I have written, one more opportunity to discover some stuff that matters greatly to me.

I'm not looking for excuses. I don't believe I am repeating myself, nor copying myself, same ole shit all over again, in this text. My goal is to revisit and reify moments of my life that haunt and form me. Form all of us. Saving stories, characters, scenes, and my reactions to them—repurposing, renovating, editing, reordering, fine-tuning, to give them another chance, another existence. New life for readers, and for me, accessible maybe in this muddle of blood and time and change we inhabit until we've forgotten it. Though it never forgets us.

I claim as a practitioner of the art of fiction the absolute prerogative to repeat myself. To practice what all other arts practice and preach. I claim this privilege because my writing belongs to me. I own it. It's me striving to salvage my story from a darker-than-dark slaveroad, from a history of floating words, floating bodies. My writing is totally mine. Me. Mine to cut up and paste, and re-paste and cut up again, performing and re-forming, representing it in as many fashions as I choose.

Mine despite copyright laws that grant to publishers the power to treat a person's writing as a form of property (as law once defined people as property) and buy that commodity from a writer. A publisher can purchase from an author the exclusive right and permission to print an author's work, and then sell that work and profit from it, as if they, the publishers, for all intents and purposes, during a stipulated period of time at least, own the work. Such transactions may support and reward writers, lead to fame and fortune, but also cage writers and writing. Define and limit the possibilities of literature's growth, its meaning. Or put another way, publishers and the book industry, empowered by law, have established a monopoly that enables them to choose what's available to the reading public. The primary value for a publisher of the right to print a book (good writing, bad writing, junk, art) becomes a book's potential to become legal tender.

THIS NOTE IS LEGAL TENDER/FOR ALL DEBTS/ PUBLIC AND PRIVATE . . . are the exact words printed on every piece of American paper money, words that Jean-Michel Basquiat collages onto his painting of a woman's face, a formal portrait, seemingly gone wrong, because B intentionally, skillfully crafts his painting to appear slapdash and clumsily executed. Bad art. The woman's face is ugly, trashy, unappealing, a seemingly amateurish, perhaps even spiteful, vindictive, nasty parody of a female face, a rendering that turns out to be not simply cruel and funny but repeats and deconstructs one of the art world's most recognizable, costly, smiling treasures—Leonardo da Vinci's portrait of a woman *aka* the *Mona Lisa.*

SAMO is warning us. Beware. Beware. Art inhabits no special category that immunizes it from the contamination and corruption of money. Everything has its price. Can be bought or sold or stripped of special allure and status. Art is bought and sold. Works of art can even become money, become legal tender. A public hungry for love, peace, understanding may line up at the door of Art, only to discover it's locked. Mona Lisa may greet us with another smile on the other side of the door, but only after we pay a fee to enter the brothel employing her.

In a marketplace where the rule is grow bigger or die, flourish or flop, neither writers nor publishers are trustworthy or beyond temptation. I insist my writing belongs to me, is mine, is me. Claim exclusive property rights. Am I a strident advocate of *property rights* only when I happen to believe the rights happen to be mine. If I were a publishing house and my next meal, my continuing existence depended on profits earned from selling my books, would I prioritize high standards or grab the money and run. My answer to such questions is yes, no, maybe. Or rather, I admit that I don't know. And I don't feel the necessity to know. Don't need to know any more than the little I already understand about property, about art, the meaning of art, meaning of commerce, the exchanges and dead ends between art and audience, between commerce and customers, between worth and price, between artists and their work, between laws and justice. I need to know nothing further than how unresolvable, irreconcilable all such vexed, unpredictable muddles always have been and will be. Especially on a slaveroad.

Anyway, writing, like all art, is doomed to fail, isn't it. Though art persists. Each art, through its own particular, recurring, stubborn medium and idioms, endeavors to create experience. To express moments experienced by an artist that have in fact vanished instantly. Unrepeatable, no longer available to be experienced again. Maybe moments never experienced, only invented or imagined. Art imitates what's missing, lost. A work of art delivers a momentary, unique bundle of sensations that may or may not be anything like what was originally perceived or expressed once upon a time by the artist. No more than a superficial resemblance to an artist's experience is apprehendable by the work's audience because, as always, moments rush together, rush past, rush away. Like unrequited love, the mystery, unattainability of art does not end its attraction, but sustains our pursuit of it.

I render copies that are both true and false, fact and fiction, copies asserting themselves, copies attempting to become (stand in for) what's ordinarily experienced, moment by moment only in the lives of living, breathing people. A task, for better or worse, beyond my power, the powers of art. Doesn't matter how compelling an experience happens to be—the experience, for instance, that compelled the artist's original attempt to render it. Art's province, its participation in the here and now of time remains inscrutable. I spin invisible words, invisible sentences written in air. In other words, a work of art tells another's story, another's life and time. An imagined reoccurrence. Yet there, surely there. Yes, yes, something's certainly there, but disappearing faster than anybody able to read it, claim it, own it. Always another's story on the page, on the canvas, in the song, in the dancing feet, in the marble. Never exactly belonging to anybody.

Reoccurrence and repetition. They reinvent one another. Cancel and complement one another. A reader can be unexpectedly transfixed by reading a piece forgotten but read before. Or readers reread by choice because they have learned there's always more to learn from a good book. Often fans are deeply disappointed when a famous band or a singer neglects to include a riff of oldies but goodies in a concert. Andy Warhol made a fortune churning out copies, and transformed the art world's perception of its business. My Pittsburgh homeboy Warhol's productions running the changes on repetition and demanding more money each time he invents a fresh way to repeat himself.

Consider him again—SAMO, Mr. Jean-Michel Basquiat, who taught himself to eavesdrop on slaveroad conversations, listening to those who pretended their hands were clean, the ones pretending to be society's guardians—cops, teachers, preachers, parents, politicians, bankers, judges, CEOs, scholars, historians, and critics of art—all trash-talking together to profit from the slaveroad's traffic. J-M Basquiat outed that ancient conversation's steady stream of only slightly disguised obscenities by repeating them in public. On New York City building walls, in his drawings and paintings. Same ole obscenities meant to ensnare, destabilize, and drown him, us. Basquiat exposed, reiterated, revised, revisited, reenvisioned, re-embodied them. Those bad-mouthing conversations reoccurring and repudiated in his artwork to save himself, free us . . .

In an email to Okey, an Igbo friend and fiction writer who had worked beside Chinua Achebe in both Nigeria and the US, I asked Okey if he knew the exact Igbo words of the proverb that Achebe had translated in *Things Fall Apart* as "all stories are true." I explained to Okey that I was starting a piece about a Virginia-born American missionary, William Henry Sheppard, who had arrived (1890) at an outpost on the Congo River at about same time Joseph Conrad had passed through—the men may even have encountered one another—before each began his separate journey upriver into what a Conrad story would call the *Heart of Darkness.* I explained to Okey that I was wondering how the Igbo proverb "all stories are true" works in Achebe's famous essay that pretty much dismisses Conrad's story as untruth.

Any help with Igbo words greatly appreciated, Okey. Might also maybe help me as I bumble along with my Sheppard story.

Okey Ndibe, who revered his esteemed elder Chinua Achebe, replied almost immediately. *Onwero akuko gb'aka*, he emailed, are the Igbo words Chinua rendered in English as "all stories are true." Okey also shared with me his own understanding of the literal meaning of those Igbo words: No story is ever empty-handed. No story is ever bereft.

William Henry Sheppard, after twenty years of service as a Presbyterian missionary in Africa, was recalled in 1910 by the church and returned home to America in disgrace. I don't want to start or end my Sheppard story there, where it ends for his contemporaries and most of us—an ending unfair to this "black Livingston," this fellow of the Royal Geographical Society, this investigator and witness who helped expose to the world the terrible crimes perpetrated by Belgian king Leopold in the Congo, this writer, lecturer William Henry Sheppard, born in Virginia, who taught himself Kuba language and art, who some Africans called "black white man," and others named Bope Mekabe because they believed him to be a reincarnation of their king's dead brother, this dreamer who attempted to establish a Congo mission, Ibaanc, run by American women and men of color, this preacher judged guilty by the Presbyterian Church of unacceptable behavior and summoned home, adultery charges against him kept quiet to spare the church embarrassment and scandal, a church whose crusade to save African souls conducted while

African bodies were enslaved and exterminated just outside of its doors, a church thus compromised morally, ethically no less than its once-upon-a-time exemplary, celebrated, then all-too-human missionary—an unfair story about this William Henry Sheppard, who was banned from preaching, close to broke when he returned to America, an outcast until the church relented and offered him a pulpit in Kentucky, where he served till he died, his fame fading, exploits nearly forgotten.

Though his wife, Lucy Gantt Sheppard, an American of color like him, joined William Henry Sheppard in the Congo (1894) and mothered three of their four children in Africa (two infant girls died of fever there; Wilhelmina survived, as did American-born William, aka Max), Sheppard confessed to Presbyterian Church officials that before and after his marriage, he had taken numerous African mistresses and acknowledged himself father of Shepete, a son born to one of those women.

Rather than vilifying or vanishing Sheppard or his misdeeds, as I learn more about him, a man whose existence unknown to me until just yesterday, until now when I am old and approaching my own end, I imagine Sheppard as a bit like me, a man beyond fearing exposure, even if not beyond guilt and shame. I imagine him looking back, as I often look back these days, at the long, crowded passage of time within each moment, the details each moment recalls. Sheppard telling his story to himself, listening to other stories without beginnings or ends, listening to words he chooses, words choosing him, words welcoming him, a long-lost brother, nearly forgotten, seeing himself again in words he thinks, makes up, speaks, words he believes he hears others say.

Unlike the church (or S himself, who in his 1917 memoir, *Presbyterian Pioneers*, records almost nothing that occurs after 1892, the year of the death of his companion and fellow missionary Samuel Norvell Lapsley—scarcely a word about Sheppard's marriage, wife, children, the Ibaanc mission staffed by missionaries of color he recruits, his popular lecture tours in America, meeting the queen of England and two United States presidents . . .), I have no reason to engage in a cover-up. No need to distance myself, pass judgment, conceal Sheppard's private life in Africa or back home. I want to write a story that sails across the Atlantic, resides in Africa for two decades, returns to America. But not a story content just to dog Sheppard's footsteps faithfully. I need a story that includes mine. Fly on the wall. My feet in Sheppard's shoes when/if they fit.

Unlike Sheppard, I grew up in Northern, not Southern states of the United States of America. But Sheppard's manner of coping with oppression feels quite familiar. He seems to have quietly accommodated himself to the strict segregation by color enforced in his region and in his Southern Presbyterian religion. He cultivated early the habit of minding his own business, often befriending when possible people not his color, ingratiating himself, thankful for their attention, praising their kindness and generosity, content to appear reconciled, undamaged by the fact that American law and custom categorize him as an inferior kind of human. Content, it would seem, to keep within himself rather than impose upon others whatever angers he might harbor. Habits of caution, survival techniques similar to ones I learned during my childhood and practiced throughout a university career. Why wouldn't S retain those same habits while a missionary in Africa. Strictly compartmentalize and discipline his feelings, his voice, his appearance. Allow others little access to his innermost thoughts. A shape-shifter adept at disguise.

Thus, no surprise to me that S not always a vocal critic of Europe's plundering of Africa—that vicious regime of forced labor, kidnapping, slavery, expropriation of land, that abyss of murder and theft surrounding him as he strove to convert Africans to believers in Christ. Yet when an international tribunal was convened in 1899 to determine if King Leopold's administration of his Congo protectorate was just and humane, information that Sheppard provided—including photos that he had risked his life to obtain, photos documenting a massacre committed by mercenaries employed by Leopold's regime—helped to discredit Leopold. Nine years later in a Southern Presbyterian newsletter, S published his eyewitness account of how a once proud and thriving Kuba kingdom was being destroyed by policies that European governments and companies deployed to loot the Congo's wealth. His testimony damning enough that one of the powerful international firms he accused, the Kasai rubber company, attempted to protect its reputation by suing S for libel.

In *Presbyterian Pioneers* S recalls a boyhood job working for a dentist he knew as Dr. Henkel. "In a back room of the . . . office was a box filled with teeth. It puzzled me much to think how in the world the people on resurrection day were to get their own teeth back."

Equally strange and puzzling for me to find S and Joseph Conrad both passed, almost simultaneously, through Matadi Station on the Congo River.

Conrad had opened an early window on Africa for me, and over the years I have often used his Congo story as a model in my creative writing classes, but not until I retired from university teaching to devote myself full time to my own fiction, and had begun to research S's career as a possible subject for a story, did I discover that S had arrived in Matadi at more or less the same moment in 1890 as Joseph Conrad. A simple historical fact on one hand, but it struck me as an uncanny coincidence, arousing my curiosity, igniting a sense of wonder. The sort of hardheaded, unsatisfiable curiosity that I believe Sheppard shares with Marlow, the fictional sailor who narrates *Heart of Darkness.*

Curiosity unsettles both Marlow and Sheppard. Drives them to take chances. Risk their lives in Africa. S's curiosity aroused by teeth. M's curiosity by rumors circulating about a Mr. Kurtz. S fascinated by the mystery of random teeth, mystery of lives lost, bones scattered and silenced forever unless one day they are reassembled and speak for themselves again. M a storyteller intrigued by a notoriously successful agent in charge of a Congo outpost, a man people feel compelled to tell tales about. Kurtz stories accumulating like teeth a dentist saves in a box. I can almost hear S and M conversing: whose teeth, whose stories once upon a time. To whom do they belong now. Asking each other why particular teeth or particular stories survive. Asking why and how do we encounter them.

And wouldn't S and M share curiosity about other mysteries. About a Second Coming, for example, or mystery of any person's living, breathing presence, here, now, girl, man, woman, boy, or ageless it seems, or at least not dead yet or perhaps already dead once and resurrected. How could anyone know, know more than rumors, stories that circulate and assert claims. Curiosity piqued by shadows scudding across dark, empty spaces inside a person's skull. Mysteries within larger mysteries. Shadows leaving behind only words, voices, silence, mysteries. Teeth.

And here we all are. Curious. Tilting with shadows. Chinua Achebe outraged by Conrad's depiction of African people, by the fact that the same old, same old African story gets told by Europeans again and again. As a kid Sheppard learning to ask questions and wondering how in the world any person answers them. Marlow the eternal, wandering outsider. Conrad a disenchanted émigré, ole boll weevil looking for a home. Me searching for an S story. All of us tellers of tales. Wanderers, immigrants, exiles, natives of more than one country, speakers of more than one language, *men* as if that idea of calling ourselves *men* means anything without the idea of *women*. All of us equal heirs of confusion, of arbitrary divisions. Pretending invented words might invent proof. As if any single word doesn't depend upon all words of all languages for meaning. As if truth of any word or story is not a daydream. Implacable sameness always bearing down. Terrorizing darkness of absolute, indistinguishable sameness. No words for it. No colors. Nothing.

To my sister, once a good Christian before she converted and became a good Muslim, I confess I am enthralled sometimes by the idea that perhaps God waits in the bottom of a bottle of good French wine. That's why I empty my glass with slow, reverent swallows, Sis, taking my time, savoring God's good time, no doubt, while I drink sip by sip, in absolutely no hurry, each individual sweet-but-not-too-bitterly-sweet sip tasting good, maybe better than the one before, maybe even sweet as the final, culminating, very last sip of all those sips getting me to the bottle's bottom, Sis, though your brother is smart enough to know that he cannot taste the last drop until the last drop comes. That last drop after which there is no more, but anyway, I tease my sister and say, it's nice to keep sipping slowly, nearer and nearer to God, to her, and if her sweet Savior not in this particular bottle, maybe the next or next, and maybe, bye-um-bye, I will hear *Well Done*, as the old folks claimed in their stories we might hear one day, or so say some people in their stories about old folks and what old folks claimed once upon a time.

It is only when we have become worthy of being created anew that we shall receive from the Good True God a new soul, full, whole. And man shall be as everlasting as God (Tokarczuk—*The Books of Jacob*).

If you are ever possessed, S, by a desire to speak, S, please describe to me in detail the session or sessions in Maryland that you were ordered to attend by your superiors in the Presbyterian hierarchy after they recalled you from Africa to America. Sessions to which you were summoned immediately, I assume, to bear witness against yourself. Confess your sins. Does an interrogation by fellow Presbyterian clerics have an official Presbyterian title—debriefing, trial, chat, inquiry, inquisition, lynching, auto-da-fé, ordeal. Given my own excruciating experience in sessions that I imagine might have been quite similar to those you were forced to endure, sessions requiring me to explain to others or myself my shameful, inexplicable behavior, I'm guessing that a single image of you—an image you saw as only one of many indistinct, changing, fleeting reflections in a dark, endless hall of mirrors—was seized upon suddenly by your judges. Examined and evaluated minutely as if sculpted in stone. Your flesh-and-blood self frozen like a body Medusa fastens her fatal gaze upon.

Sheppard and his fellow missionary Samuel Norvell Lapsley, like Conrad's Mr. Kurtz, steam and paddle deeper and deeper into the primeval forest, searching for an outpost, for willing souls, for fertile ground where civilization might lay down its burden of history and start fresh. Enrich itself. Re-enlighten and un-doom itself. Kurtz a believer. A sort of missionary, not unlike Sheppard and Lapsley and Rebekah. A man stirred by the notion of a higher calling, the possibility of constructing a better world. And though K, like Conrad, probably too intelligent, too jaded to think anyone, anywhere will ever truly achieve or inhabit such a world, K believes a better world, empty or not, should be humankind's goal. Believes that a better, more prosperous future will materialize if and only if a determined, ruthless few seek it relentlessly, and with absolutely no compromises. A dedicated few, conscious like K of their duty, of a higher calling, must articulate through their lives and work an impossible world, a world in which no one could ever live day by day, day after day, but a place the elect (writers of stories?) must strive to envision and demand.

A perfect world, perfect story. Is perfection K's goal: a purified marketplace of never-ending, escalating profit. Like perfect models that fiction writers and poets of older generations sought to construct and pass on. A perfect imitation, though centuries ago Plato, unconvinced, railed against such recklessness. Predicted dire consequences for humankind's grasp of reality when art's imitations compete with nature's productions.

A friend asked me recently, "What does your writing say. What does it teach. What do you want to leave behind for young people coming up after you."

I was speechless. Embarrassed. Outed for a fraud. No answer possible. Better to ignore or forget my friend's unfriendly questions.

Weeks later, unable to fall asleep one night after rereading notes in my journal for an unfinished story, I found myself jotting down a few "propositions," not to respond directly to the friend's questions, nor to prove anything in particular, just a few propositions (I still call them propositions because I can't come up with a better word) to express what I hope readers and writers who pay careful attention to my work might find. On that restless night reciting, reiterating, a chorus addressing myself or maybe just a broken record repeating over and over my uncertain intentions, my wishful thinking about what and why I write, whom I address, what I struggle to embody in fiction, I finally scratch into my journal: *words dance—silence speaks—language is music—music dreams.*

Did you, Sheppard, ever admit to your wife, Lucy Gantt Sheppard, the trespasses that you confessed to Presbyterian Church officials. If/when Sheppard tells Lucy Gantt Sheppard stories of his betrayals of her, does he share her suffering. One story. Many. Would Sheppard suffer more telling his tales of trespass to Lucy Gantt Sheppard or to the Presbyterian clerics.

What Achebe particularly disapproves in his essay critiquing Conrad's Congo story, what outrages Achebe most about *Heart of Darkness*, I think, is the safety net Conrad provides for reasonable Englishmen, for himself, for us. Like Marlow, the character he creates to narrate *HOD*, Joseph Conrad supplies a soothing cover-up. Marlow lies. Readers watch M lie to K's intended bride. Lie and deceive when he doesn't tell K's bride-to-be that K's last words to him were: *the horror, the horror.* M lies even though he declares he hates and detests lies. And yes, like M, the rest of us would probably profess quite strongly that we believe lying is wrong. But hold on, wait a minute, JC's story says to readers. Is M really such a bad bloke, after all. Too gloomy sometimes, maybe. Maybe too ready to pop off to exotic, faraway places with strange-sounding names. Maybe too prone to get himself mixed up in business way above his pay grade, but not that awful a guy, is he? Are we?

Africa is a godforsaken, hopeless place. Isn't that the problem, the point Conrad makes. Marlow a hard worker, likes his pint, a decent chap, not a bad lad, not much worse than most of us, is he. Feels pity for the poor darkies now and again, don't he. And can't we forgive a fella a wee bit of a fib to soothe a damsel in distress. Besides, the fib keeps her happy, right. And after all, Marlow confesses the lie to his mates, don't he. And lie or not, isn't M an entertaining storyteller. We would be sitting here bored stiff, stuck between tides on the Thames without M's company. He spins a good yarn, doesn't he. A good lad. A good read, after all.

I can hear Achebe interrogating Joseph Conrad. Where does your story take place? Africa, you say? Whose Africa? Who says so? Whose dark heart explored? Exposed? Who is lying? Why?

When Achebe's eyes caught mine that day in Amherst, Massachusetts, I saw a look from him intently directed at me. Not aggressive, not lasting very long, yet intense, expressive, a glance that plainly said, "I believe or rather hope, my new acquaintance, hope you know better than the remarks you just chattered to brighten the conversation."

Chinua Achebe's eyes met mine across a white, wrought iron table, at which we sat with a mutual friend, Mike Thelwell, a Jamaican writer who had brought us together. In them I read equal amounts of worry, wary distance, weariness, distaste, pity. I don't remember what I said to provoke the look—perhaps we were discussing Conrad's famous story in my backyard, I called a *garden*, but I have never forgotten Chinua Achebe's look, my embarrassment and shame, a blot upon my first encounter with him that haunts me, that blot and another: the bottle of decent scotch whiskey I chose to serve that late afternoon in Amherst before I had read Achebe's fiction and knew him only by reputation as an "acclaimed African writer," the scotch we drank that day because for benighted me, any acclaim granted an "African" author of fiction suspect, and did not necessarily signify superior writing, so this "Achebe" didn't necessarily deserve the very best bottle I had to offer.

By the time I met Achebe in Amherst, Jimmy Baldwin, also in residence there, was lecturing in one of the country's pioneering Afro-American Studies departments. Similar programs at other schools were being inaugurated, recruiting writers and scholars of color. Still, abysmal ignorance of African history, cultures, politics, ignorance of the African global diaspora, the suffering, transformation, and glories of African-descended peoples everywhere on the planet, continued to reign in academia. A reign of ignorance plus arrogance, since according to many academics, any African story, missing or not in traditional university curricula, couldn't really amount to very much.

Little changed until some of us began to understand that we were victims as much as we were beneficiaries of an educational system which had chosen long ago to omit crucial information about us. A brutal choice that marginalized, stigmatized, or rendered us invisible. With missionary zeal some of us embarked upon crusades to transform our universities. Enlighten the heathen. Uproot, expose, illuminate lies and misrepresentations that marginalized our humanity.

Like WHS when he set off for the Congo, many of us believed we were responding to a higher calling. Though few of us had ever heard of S, we imitated him assiduously, without being aware that we followed his example. S sporting a pith helmet, white puttees, white linen suit in the Congo. My brethren and I sporting three-piece Brooks Brothers suits, rep ties, dapper in Stacy Adams shoes.

Displaying ourselves conspicuously on campus in costumes associated with people not our color. Our elegant dress and speech were beguiling, unexpected mysteries calculated to seize the natives' attention, keep them enthralled. Though some of us did prefer to mau-mau the savages, strutted around in robes and turbans or mimicked hippie, half-naked funk and disarray, cussing out our pupils with polyglot ghetto profanities, scaring, cowing them (and college administrators) into submission. Convert or else.

Just yesterday I learned from an essay, perhaps written by a Bakete speaker, that the title bestowed on S, Mudele Ndome, doesn't necessarily mean "black whiteman," but rather signifies "man clothed as people not us clothe themselves."

Crucial information, crucial perspectives omitted from *HOD*, Achebe believes, so he supplies them in his essay about the story. Invents a photo of JC. And why would I deny my elder, better brother Chinua Achebe a license I will later grant to myself as this story continues. Of course, Achebe doesn't need my permission nor anybody else's permission to tell stories, to tell readers his JC story. He takes a snapshot of Conrad, and offers it as a portrait of JC, like it or lump it. Here's an unpleasant likeness of JC, Achebe declares, and accepts full responsibility for presenting it. Exactly the sort of responsibility he asks JC to take for the kind of Africans and Africa that JC fabricates through an opaque partnership with M. And if A refuses to grant JC a reprieve for not thoroughly, consistently clarifying an authorial point of view distinct from the point of view of his creation, Marlow, or from Kurtz or from the factors, enslavers, executioners of Congolese people—who is in a position, who possesses the moral authority to prove Achebe wrong.

When do stories become cover-ups. Are writers responsible for aiding and abetting crimes when, knowingly, they tell tales that conceal crimes. Do writers become self-serving accomplices to crime even if a fiction or lie they tell is motivated by good intentions. With a Marlow serving up a big lie to protect her, would Lucy Gantt Sheppard suffer any more or less than K's intended.

Who listens to suffering's ever-present wails. Who is wailing. Who suffers. Who profits. The story, the autobiography I want Sheppard stories, Rebekah stories to help me construct could start there. Not by supplying answers. Art at best a feeble address to suffering. No story prevents fresh suffering, removes old bloodstains from our hands. Still, Achebe demands that stories, including JC's stories, address their debt, address the slaveroad, the suffering from which they arise.

You departed by canoe the Congo mission you had helped to establish, S, accompanied by African porters, arming them as you were armed with modern European guns. The porters were from the interior, Africans you recruited because they claimed to be more familiar with the perilous wilderness upriver than the locals. You were determined, I learned from *Presbyterian Pioneers*, to enter Kuba territory and search for the legendary ruler of the Kuba kingdom, determined to find the hidden, secret compound where, enthroned upon a sacred, royal stool, he reigned. Determined, though warned by fellow missionaries, government officials, merchants, traders, African Christians whom the mission served, that Kuba land forbidden, that outsiders who entered their territory without permission were considered trespassers by the Kuba, a crime condemning trespassers to unspeakable deaths.

Driven, I assume, by what you perceived as the holiness of your task—freeing African souls from ignorance entombing them—you decided to seek assistance from the most powerful Kuba king to forward your mission. Undeterred by any threat to your personal safety, you, along with your porters and your baggage, boarded a long canoe rowed by African converts enlisted from the mission's flock, and departed for Kuba territory. But after two days of rough going, fighting white water, treacherous portages through nearly impassable jungle, risking the canoe in tributaries without knowing exactly the direction in which the water might meander or whether water would remain deep enough to float a loaded canoe to more water it could navigate, the rowers' courage was exhausted.

I wonder if their fledgling souls deserted them. Wonder if S wondered. Was S disappointed. By them. Disappointed by himself. By the soul's fragility. Had he failed the African converts. Did they listen to him without hearing him. All that praying, hymn singing, and now, tested, his new Christian converts had faltered. Chosen to cling to life in a fallen world, rather than risk doing God's work. Didn't they understand God's gift. Understand the rapture of letting go. Relying totally on His mercy, His promise of life everlasting in a world of no toil, no troubles. That glorious world S had labored to describe in his mission sermons. That peaceable kingdom reachable by faith and good deeds in this cruel one. Did S wonder if his clumsy words, in a clumsy language he invented and cobbled together as he spoke, had failed to convince, or were these Africans simply refusing to go further into country unknown to them, unknown except as home to merciless beasts and merciless beast men, hostile, violent, beyond dangerous, another country like the country living in the hearts of foreigners who arrived from across the seas.

In *Presbyterian Pioneers* you wrote that you didn't try to dissuade the rowers. Thanked them, blessed them. Wished them Godspeed as they began to paddle the mission's long canoe back in the direction from which you had come.

I'm trying hard to imagine what you imagined you might achieve, S, by continuing your trek to save souls. How could you think that you might find the king you were seeking. A king it was said his subjects venerated more as a deity than as a monarch. Even if by some extraordinarily lucky chance you stumbled upon his sacred city, and even if some even more unlikely piece of luck landed you in his royal presence and he permitted you to stand or kneel or grovel before him, what exactly did you intend to say to the Kuba king, S. And if your extraordinary string of good luck continued and the king commanded you to speak, how would you understand his words. Speak his language. Beyond a few words and phrases picked up from other missionaries or your African congregation.

Were you truly a holy fool, S. Did you anticipate divine intervention or a divinely inspired translator. How in the world did you expect that a handful of Kuba words, if you could summon up even a few, and even if a haughty monarch was amused by hearing those few words mangled by your foreigner's tongue, how did you believe you might convince him to approve, let alone support or encourage your effort to establish a new, a rival god in the Kuba kingdom. A god who sends you, a pale, mumbling, pith-helmeted emissary, to spread His word. To preach the message of His omnipotence. Describe glorious treasures He wishes to shower upon Kuba people.

Did a quiet part of you, S, a part almost totally submerged by your fierce drive, your Christian duty to convert and save African souls, did it ever whisper to you, S, remind you, S, that you were driven also because you were still seeking, still desiring, still hungry, still lacking, still awaiting conversion's promise of peace. Perhaps you would pray sometimes just barely loud enough you hoped for your God to hear or not to hear, a prayer that you might discover conversion's secret, learn it there, live it there. Your soul at rest among those darker, mysterious strangers.

On the second day of wandering, lost absolutely in jungled wilderness, your hired porters' alleged familiarity with the terrain vanished, gone perhaps like the rowers' belief in a life everlasting, lost there, lost, lost, lost, suddenly, you are hailed and halted by a motley crew of armed men. A party of those roving, raiding marauders everyone on the coast feared: thieves, slavers, murderers of children and women, occasional mercenaries, killers who would slaughter people simply for pleasure.

To the leader of that crew you must have seemed like a gift. Strangers—a black/white man in an odd costume accompanied by his slaves. Slaves bearing guns and baggage on their shoulders, bags gripped in their fists. Slaves stooped under the weight of their loads. Copious sacks, boxes, bundles containing, no doubt, precious possessions of their master. Unexpected bounty encountered deep in the forest. Wandering fools, lost souls. Merchandise belonging now to the marauder. Booty to be sold, traded. Bodies to be eaten, if no better offers arose. Unless Kuba scouts interfered and chose to torture, behead, drape your corpses in trees, a warning to other violators of Kuba territory.

Yes, yes. Follow us, I can hear the words of the guerrilla band's leader. Visualize him pantomiming his offer. We will guide you to the king. The king loves me. Only a three days' march to his compound, and lucky for you, we are headed there. Lucky you found us to guide you through dangerous territory many enter, but few return. Follow us, if you please, he said. Said in what language. What language of eloquent gesticulations, eyes flashing, fingers pointing. Or maybe a language spoken by one of your porters. In no language would the leader of the pack of scavengers say to you, Guns or no guns, you must sleep. And when you do sleep, my swift vultures will dive into your dreams. Snatch guns. Snatch you. Guns worth much more than your bodies.

Follow behind us, he would say. And of course, since it appeared you had no better option, you and the porters fell in behind the raiders, struggling to keep up with their rapid pace, trailing them mile after mile.

But yes, you were lucky. Damned lucky, S. That's one sure thing I can say about you. Despite troubles and trials and tribulations and disappointments and failures, you, like me, are a survivor. Like me, S, one lucky motherfucker.

Just before nightfall of the day you hooked up with the raiding party, night falling there in the depths of the forest, an abrupt, black, black total eclipse, no sunlight, no moonlight, and one of the last sights visible to you a clearing not many yards ahead where the path beneath your feet seemed to intersect with another path cutting through thick undergrowth, both paths tunneling through an impenetrable jungle, passages roofed by unbroken canopies of foliage, a sort of crossroads intersection opening in dense bush where you found yourself, and you knowing that what you had just glimpsed would be absolutely unseeable in a minute or two, but then, as you crossed the clearing to enter the pathway you had barely discerned up ahead, you, your two terrified porters, and the outlaws you had been following for hours, the long file of all of you suddenly collapses, and you are bunched together, herded, huddled together by many, many Africans, naked Africans who had materialized from utter darkness surrounding the clearing, Africans quietly, in an encompassing, enclosing semicircle.

Palavering, probably much pointing, many gestures mostly invisible to you in the darkness, but not lasting long. One preemptory voice clearly giving orders. In a few moments the band of raiders and their chief regrouped, hustled away, into the darkness, and though most of the Africans and their weapons remained invisible, did you sense them closer, closer, S. Did torches or lanterns suddenly illuminate the scene in front of you. A dull, wavering glow backlighting bodies emerging from the bush, bodies substantial, insubstantial as shadows, forms moving silent as ghosts who forced the porters to their knees and stripped from them and distributed among themselves and their invisible companions everything the porters had been carrying. The African intruders kicked and pummeled the porters while unburdening them, and I see the two men you'd hired, almost naked now themselves, and they do not attempt to stand again, but crouch, roll, crawl, raise their arms, flail, plead for mercy, as if drowning in the high, wild, black sea of grass and bush where they landed, cowering there until prodded by African spears and they bolt up, stagger, disappear into the night, in the direction, they must be hoping, from which our party had arrived.

Torches, lanterns extinguished. You have a new leader, S. Alone beside him in unyielding dark. He must be the one who set the trap, ordered the violent confiscation of your baggage, the mauling, beatings, the one whose shout halted kicks and battering and freed the porters to rise and hobble off. He informs you he is your new leader by smiling, maybe, a big smile, big, pointed, yellow teeth caught half a second in a slash of light from some unknown source, or perhaps his face simply so close to yours you believed you must be able to see and smell his cannibal teeth and so you did, and they were part of the smile, palpable as the unseen fingers on your elbow urging, edging you gently to fall in line again with this new leader, a high chief, king's counselor, you would learn later, him letting you understand you must follow his warriors. Through darkness impenetrable without them and their weapons, their leader leading them and leading you.

How long did you stay away, S. Remain a guest in the Kuba king's compound, a favorite of the Kuba king, feted by some of the king's kinsmen as ghost of the king's long-dead brother.

Did you become magically fluent in a new language. Discovering, admiring, stunned by the king's wealth, the art of his people, their sculptures, the colorful, intricate designs decorating fabrics they wove, the endless variety of their songs, dances, the age and subtlety of their rituals. The culture and artifacts surrounding the king unexpected wonders for you, and your immersion in them deeper and deeper, S, until the king tires of you, or exotique you no longer serve for the king whatever purposes you once had served squatting on a rug beside him while he ruled astride his royal stool. Or you tire of him, or all of the above, and then, escorted by Kuba warriors, a long journey back home, where, once again, upon your arrival you are received as if risen from the dead. This time not by the Kuba, but by your wife and your colleagues at the mission.

LAPSLEY

Among those joyful, maybe a bit bemused, incredulous folk greeting the ghost of you at the mission station, none perhaps more enthusiastic, grateful, more relieved, more excited by your return, S, than Samuel Norvell Lapsley. Lapsley your fellow missionary, fellow Southerner and fellow Southern Presbyterian, companion on your journey from America to Africa. SNL, who had been placed in charge of the projected Congo mission, his color a necessary condition. No mission on the dark continent in the 1890s conceivable by the Southern Presbyterian missionary board unless headed by a man of Lapsley's color. No Presbyterian mission in Africa during numerous years you had petitioned the church to send you there, Sheppard. Mission impossible until church officials found a man of the appropriate color, a white leader for colored you to follow.

This Samuel Norvell Lapsley—born and raised in Selma, Alabama, father a staunch segregationist, a judge, an elder in the Presbyterian Church—SNL once stirred my curiosity nearly as much as you did, Sheppard. I was distracted (enthralled—enslaved) for a moment by the thought that I might discover lots about myself by studying a person whose background differed profoundly from mine. Discover even more than I would from studying the background of a person like you, S, similar to mine.

A dumb thought. My idea quickly runs into a wall, doesn't it. Any version of myself, any versions of you, S, or Rebekah or Achebe or Conrad or SNL that I create, are equally figments of my imagination. Equally fictions. Lives of others impenetrable, and the past unrecoverable. Not reproducible. Beyond comprehension. Except as wishful thinking, magical thinking. What counts is each moment. What matters is the story in which I momentarily reside, the person's story momentarily residing in me. Self-consciousness of being.

An SNL story could begin with that missing photo I desire of Sheppard and Lapsley. Ocular proof of the two men's height and size relative to one another. The photo would help us, you and me, to walk through this story, as if it reads itself aloud, does not require writing more words, reading words again I've written already, testing again the truth of them, truth of us.

L much smaller than S in the photo I must invent, invent since digitized archives accessible to me do not seem to contain the image I need to illustrate my story. An odd fact because archived photo albums hold plenty of pictures of S posing with others—an eight-foot-long python, a water buffalo, fellow missionaries, African women, African laborers, elaborately costumed warriors, crowds of dark naked children, a camel, snapshots and formal portraits of S with his wife and kids, with African converts, with visitors from neighboring tribes, from Europe. A lavish gallery of faces and bodies displayed in S's photo albums to illustrate his busy life and adventures, but no photo of S and SNL together, standing, sitting, posed casually or formally, and I can't help wondering why. The omission too obvious to be accidental, to go unnoticed by S or L.

Despite obvious differences, they are great friends. In writing left behind, each man speaks highly of the other. Daily companions. Worked, played, prayed together. "Thank God for S," L exclaimed in a letter to his parents. Side by side, S and L confronted dangerous wild animals, hostile waterways, hostile native tribes. Nursed each other through bouts of malaria. Cleaned up the other's vomit, piss, shit. Sweating together when the jungle temperature too high to register on a thermometer, "swimming wet as ducks in a puddle," as one or the other put it, under six blankets fellow missionaries piled on top of them to break a deadly fever.

Where are the photos that must've been taken to celebrate, to commemorate the special bonding of S and L, their survival despite the odds. A camera available it seemed from their first Congo days. But usually only the two of them, not counting Africans, manning the station, so if either one operated the camera, perhaps I shouldn't expect both to be framed in a photo. Still, there are plenty of solo shots of S, none of L preserved in albums in the Presbyterian archive. Why not. Is L camera shy, fussy about having his picture taken. Or maybe huge-ego S, too busy posing, never thinks of asking his partner to pose. And why am I speculating about an absent photo, creating a mystery that may exist only because I invent it? A clear violation of my storytelling license. Like claiming in my narrative to see the photo I desire but in fact did not find. Photo showing S much taller, broader than L. Both men captured in the same blink of a camera eye.

The face of SNL appears in *Presbyterian Pioneers* and also in a volume of L's correspondence and diary entries collected and published (1893) by his family after L's death. A very different face greets you, however, depending upon which of those books you consult. Fine, almost delicate features, a young, attractive, sensitive individual, most viewers would probably agree, this L who I see in a full-page formal portrait S chooses for his memoir. L boyish.

Clean-cheeked, bare upper lip. A face innocent and vulnerable. Eyes that don't quite meet the reader's eyes directly. In the photo his relatives picked to introduce his life and letters, L gazes right, almost in profile, with his lip, cheeks adorned by the elegant drop of a grown-up's mustache. Face more mature, mysterious than the face of L that S offers his readers. Two views of the missing partner. No doubt L present in both. But mystery of his absence, if mystery it is, from photo albums that document S's African adventures not solved, perhaps even deepens.

I don't need to be told everything. But do want my chance to listen. Want my chance to tell.

The missing photo might also show whose skin is lighter or darker than the other's. It would not show color. Color banished from old photos unless restored by technology. Kodak pictures from the 1890s in their pebble-grained fashion indicate only a multitude of shades and gradations of light. We can't see colors in the photos, only imagine them, as once upon a time we pretended to see colors on screens of black-and-white TV sets. Physics defines color as visible light reflected by a specific wavelength. Thus, black and white, according to physics, are both absolutes. Black conveying total absence of anything to see. White conveying too much of everything to see. Eyes blinded by absolutes. Colors disappear. Thus, *black* and *white*—when employed to designate a person's color—are stipulations, culturally assigned labels. The skin colors black or white that we claim to see, claim to recognize, that appear to us shimmering, real, reassuring, are there and not there. Black and white are colors imagined, not seen. Colors not definable by wavelength. Except as absolute boundaries of the visible. Each time we claim to see a black Sheppard, a white Lapsley, we are pretending. We are blind on the slaveroad. Seeing people who are not there, ghosts produced by wishful thinking, dreams, nightmares, hallucinations, mirrors, stories.

L's correspondence and diary record his fascination, his changing notions of skin color. On their way to Africa, touring London with S, L seems surprised that the color of S's skin doesn't automatically restrict an English person's perceptions of S's social mobility. L notices that a man of S's color at a concert, tea party, or museum doesn't appear to ruffle people's expectations. The English, SNL remarks, don't notice at all what seems very odd to us.

Once settled in the Congo, SNL grows "used to black faces or rather black bodies" of Africans surrounding him. "Just like our own darkies," he says. Color, he says, "made me feel quite at home." SNL is even able to crack a color joke and make fun of the absurdity of labeling a person either black or white: "white man as they call S."

L notices more. More than black or white. Notices more and more of the unseen. Notices that putting himself on notice in Africa produces weight. Weight of noticing more world. A world the words *black* and *white* conceal. Notices the negative weight of vanity in a man who wishes to annul himself, abdicate himself absolutely in service of his God. Notices vanity of the notion of his own importance, of inserting his "white" color, his "white" words, eyes, ears, every sense white and alert at the center of whatever circumstance in which he finds himself. As if his white notice, his attention, his recording of what transpires around him matters inordinately.

He notices the vanity of basking in the praise of his peers and family back home in Alabama when they remark upon his "poet's sensibility, painter's eye" in his descriptions of nature. Weight of vanity he notices and is able to temper only slightly by telling himself he's working diligently to accurately picture this Africa in letters home, not to aggrandize himself, but for the benefit of others who will never experience the beauty and strangeness and weight of an Africa he sees daily.

He draws maps. Records words of native languages in his journals. Shyly he notices the African way of squatting. Men and women nearly naked, bottoms almost in contact with the ground, bare thighs splayed, legs steepled, knees wide apart. A position Africans assume and can maintain almost indefinitely, it seems. Notices women squatting in the mission yard all day as they work and chatter. Notices they don't give a thought to the outrageous immodesty of a habitual posture he considers surely obscene, remarkably lewd at first as their lewd public dancing, until he notices that like them, he can take the display for granted, and notice and appreciate the eloquent dances, appraise agile bodies, graceful limbs, the workmanship of aprons, a woven cloth or occasional flap of dyed animal skin, aprons fore and aft, secured by a string women tie around their waist.

Two flaps and a string, he notices, the sole garment of grown-up women busy about the yard in the next to nothing covering them well enough, they surely believe, and, he notices, as they squat, scraggles of hair and various creases punctuating the women's soft bottom parts poised just inches above the dirt or grass. Notices he couldn't always quite keep himself from thinking about these always hungry women's bottoms as they squatted. Were nether lips foraging, feeding on grubs in the mud or bits of vegetation or lips parting to relieve a swollen belly or bowels evacuating or spewing out babies and yet he also notices that in a surprisingly short time he became accustomed absolutely to absolutely naked little girls or their aproned mothers squatting before him, conversing with him, him busy filling notebooks with examples of their Kete words and phrases, setting aside his fanciful pictures of what hidden lips might be performing, noticing instead animated features of dark faces, their white eyes, white teeth, agile lips pronouncing Bakete for him to learn.

Notices that sometimes he still forgets his modesty as he watches a woman sway with that characteristic alternation of wobble and metronomic swing of sturdy hump above bare legs, legs often thin, long, he notices, skinny legs, dancing the mound of flesh above them, and he wonders again about the action concealed by flaps of apron when a woman stands, walks, or squats, but those pursed lips or nibbling mouths, those secrets, whatever they might be, absolutely none of his business, of course, and noticing his lingering indecency, he would have to caution himself, repeat to himself the mantra "mind your own business, SNL." Yes, yes, but how to ignore those swaying hips, those perfect clocks wound just tight enough to keep perfect time till the end of time and beyond.

SNL earns a new name. Ntomanjela, his Bakete friends, then all Africans at the Luebo mission, begin to call him. Ntomanjela, meaning "pathfinder," because they believe Ntomanjela is finding a way into their country, their homes, their language, and their hearts.

SNL notices a woman asking S, "God you talk to, Sheppard, and you say talk to you and talk to Ntomanjela and love you and you say you love him and he love us, Sheppard, how he our god and not know our words, our names."

SNL notices the incredible varieties here in this Congo jungle of flora and fauna, of colors and landscapes and waterways and weather and skies and tribes. Notices more of Sheppard. And L notices if he is patient and studies a fly just landed on the back of his hand, the fly will often freeze, and if he outpatients it, the insect will eventually stir, wiggle a leg, a wing before beginning to crawl, a preparatory minuscule dance before it explores or bites him, and precisely then, while the fly intent on its business, L could swat it, kill it with great proficiency he had noticed back when he was a boy in Alabama, and notices with great wonder and some pride how the same kind of patience, same old boyhood trick he taught himself and mastered, works here too.

In his *Presbyterian Pioneers* memoir S adroitly employs a variety of narrative devices that allow him to approach in his writing as close to L's color, as close to L as he dares. A formal letter of mourning addressed to L's mother after S learns of his partner's death permits S to frame, to conventionalize an intimate outpouring of grief and love. Throughout his memoir, his curiosity about the difference and attraction of L's skin color is not presented as a personal reaction, but recorded as the response, the fascination of naive African eyes:

> ... anxious to see his feet. They begged and pleaded with him—men, women and children—to pull off ... his socks they called bags, that they might get one peep at least. To satisfy the crowd Mr. Lapsley exhibited his small, clean, white feet. The eyes of the people opened wide. They laughed, talked and pulled at each other, so pleased. Then they got on their knees and began to handle them. Mr. Lapsley was ticklish under the bottoms of his feet and this caused him to join in with the admirers in a hearty laugh. This exhibition had to be repeated for the newcomers a number of times daily.

Invariably, out of habit, respect, conditioning by the Southern tradition in which he was raised, or perhaps a desire not to offend readers and sponsors who, no doubt, would be L's color, not his, S always addresses L (the excerpt above no exception) as *Mr. Lapsley* in his Congo book. That deadpan, unchanging formality starts to become funny to this reader. Silly, like those ever-present black anklets on naked men's feet in old porno flicks.

Mr. L performing a crowd-pleasing display of his color for Africans is the first "unseen sight" in a section of his memoir S titles: "Six Unseen Sights." But yes, certainly, S does see. He is a member of L's audience and unapologetically participates. Similar performances are repeated often, it seems, and S witnesses those as well. Though

L's unveiling of his feet, unveiling of his color resembles striptease to me, S suggests no unsavoriness. None of the provocation, eroticism, voyeurism, objectification, commodification, homoeroticism that striptease threatens and risks. The performance of L, and the reaction of his curious African audience, get a free pass. S included.

The sight of L sharing his small, clean, white feet turns out to be one of *Presbyterian Pioneer*'s best moments. S clearly enjoys it. The mood is uncritical, high-spirited, one of the happiest, most carefree scenes in the entire memoir. L's color clearly a blessing. Yet another gift, another bounty and mystery missionaries bring to the Congo. L exposing himself to the gaze of innocent African eyes complements numerous other depictions by S of proper clean fun he and L explore together innocently: "We would swim . . . to a large sand bank . . . and on the warm sand would enjoy hand over hand and leap frog and run races."

Does Sheppard remember a square of yellowish red earth, a patch of stomped-down, dried mud in the mission yard serving as a blackboard, and SNL presiding over it, preaching, holding a long stick of bamboo, drawing a large letter *A* in the dirt, and pronouncing the letter's sound four, five, six times, then with bamboo stick, words, gestures, grimaces, and smiles, L gently prompting a crowd of African children to repeat an *A* sound after him. At first the children's response a mottled array of sounds, a mixture of many versions of the sound *ah* for the letter *A* that L had pronounced. But different *ah*s imitating L's voice were also harmonized, rhythmic, blending spontaneously, subtle as Bach counterpoint, because the children, though speakers of various languages, share a common culture that predisposes and guides them to sync their different voices into song. The first few repetitions of *ah*, even if clearly not exactly what L desired from his pupils, were musical, and gradually, quickly really, given the number of different sounds from different mouths—*has—ah—a—Ahs—Haas—a-a*—after a few ensemble recitations patiently elicited by L's stick tapping the letter and repeating his *ah* sound again and again, the voices evolve into a single ah that must match perfectly in L's mind the sound of the letter in his mouth, in the dirt, because he smiles. The children's seamless unanimity pleasing to him, *ah, ah, ah*, as he listens to one sound replicated over and over flawlessly. One voice. Lots of dark, skinny, naked, hungry, dying children happy learning, and L happy—*ah-ah-ah*—and S watching him perhaps and perhaps happy too, watching happy L almost prancing at the end of the stick that had traced the letter *A* in a dried patch of mud.

On an April night in 1891, in a campsite on the north bank of the Lulua River, a tributary of the Congo, William Henry Sheppard and Samuel Norvell Lapsley, two young American men in their twenties, newcomers to Africa searching for a location where a Presbyterian mission might flourish, find themselves overwhelmed by vast, all-encompassing darkness, sheer isolation, and strangeness of being unimaginably far from home, far from people who speak their language. Only howls of jackals, screams of macaws breaking jungle stillness, S writes, and writes that in a tent their African porters have set up, the two missionaries sob audibly, cling to each other.

I can't keep myself from flashing backwards two centuries before that moment in a tent in Africa that S describes, flash back to a plantation in a country yet to name itself and declare its independence from England. I imagine two young men, newly arrived there after many weeks sick, hungry, chained, crossing an ocean surrounded by others in chains, confined in the closeness of a stinking ship's fetid hold with many, many others sick, dying, hungry, pissing, shitting, vomiting, moaning, African children, women, and men, a Babel of languages, except all speak the tongue of suffering, and hearing that unending, suffering voice again at night in a slave hovel in a

New World overwhelms two young men who sob audibly, reach out to touch one another, men captured by slavers raiding their villages, marched in coffles to the sea, sea a slaveroad crossed to a land shrouded in all-encompassing darkness, night or day, sheer loneliness, sheer strangeness of an unimaginable distance from home, from people who speak their tongue. Only snarls and cracking whips of masters in this terrifying Virginny, masters absolutely as unworthy of service as S and L believe the Master they chose to serve is infinitely worthy of service.

LUCY GANTT SHEPPARD

Stories gone missing. Absent like the missing photo I searched for. Photo of S and L standing side by side. Or the missing story of Rebekah. Or the missing story of you, Lucy Gantt, who married Sheppard.

Lucy Gantt Sheppard, like you, Rebekah, lost two children while she pursued her mission. But truth is, many children die, their mothers dedicated to a sacred mission or not. Lots of infants, lots of young children die soon, too soon, countless children die always, though of course, of course, no matter how many children die, of course, of course, one of yours dying, each one, every time kills you, explodes your heart, the unbearable shattered pieces irreplaceable, scattering, flying, creeping away, how long, how long. Death of Anna Maria, Rebekah's first child an even deeper heartbreak, if deeper possible, not only because Anna Maria died and killed R's dreams for her baby, but also because R feared her daughter's fear. Anna Maria dying and buried among strangers in a foreign land where Rebekah must abandon her. No family nor friends, no generations to greet A M, to welcome her. So Rebekah feared Anna Maria would forever be inconsolably afraid, lonely, very lonely, buried in an untended yard behind an abandoned church, in a patch of earth just before row after row of clumsy hills begin to climb towards distant mountains, the ground cold in fall and winter, ground covered season after season by snow and ice. No one there for A M to talk to, no one to talk to her, quiet her fear, mourn her, help her forget the terrible shortness of her life.

Rebekah had a second daughter, who she also named Anna Maria, her second child, last child, whose father she had met and married after her first husband, ailing Matthau Freundlich, dies, then his ailing daughter dead also, just months after the family crossed the Atlantic from St. Thomas, father, mother, daughter on the slaveroad, hoping for health, recuperation in Europe.

I met Rebekah's second little girl in a painting by Johann Valentin Haidt, a talented, inquisitive European man who emigrated from Europe and lived many years among Moravian missionaries on St. Thomas before returning and residing in Moravian communities in Germany. Rebekah, her second husband, Christian Jacob Protten, and their daughter, the second Anna Maria, posing for Haidt in Germany. An almost holy family kind of portrait, revealing how lovingly the Berlin-born painter's brush, his eye dwell on their faces, their thoughts. Haidt enlivening them, saving them. The painter's invisible hand as tender and worshipful as R's hand, visible in the painting, a hand that H includes though it violates slightly the integrity of R's body, stretching her arm rather further than a natural arm could stretch. Haidt stretching the rules of perspective, so R's arm juts impossibly through the picture plane to reach from the shadowed background into the foreground, enabling her long fingers gently to touch her daughter A M's elbow.

Did R name her second daughter to reanimate the first, to soothe loss perhaps, and soothe her fear of her first daughter's fear. The loneliness of being bereft and deserted. Perhaps in the new body of a new daughter A M could be cherished again, renewed by an identical name, *Anna Maria*. A life started over, a reoccurrence. But it didn't, doesn't last, does it. Her life stops abruptly again.

Yet maybe the painting a kinder cemetery for A M. This very young girl with bushy, reddish hair I stare at, her skin lighter than R's medium-brown skin, lighter than quite light Protten's skin in the painting I saw first in black and white in a book, then in color on the internet, scrolling to the picture many times, gazing at it and attempting to form my own picture of each of them. A trinity. The painting almost a religious relic, preserving the faces of R's family, but I know very well the moment of peace didn't last. Probably less than a year after they sat for the Haidt portrait, the family grieving again. A M gone again. A second daughter, buried in a foreign land. The beloved name R had chosen for her, the name Anna Maria that she hoped might give a second chance for life to her first daughter, didn't save the second one.

Of course children die, lots and lots die, but of course, if it's your child dying, what's it matter how many others dying, the endless, brutal, countless number of children dying, when you must, on a cold spring day in 1752, bury your precious A M again.

I wonder if Lucy Gantt Sheppard still possesses the letter from Sheppard inviting her, drawing her to Africa. Letter she awaited ten years. Number of years more or less that Kurtz's intended awaited a letter from K summoning her to Africa. Or is the long-awaited letter from S missing. Missing like the photo of S and L side by side, a photo I'm still searching for. Missing like the last words of Kurtz—*the horror, the horror*. Words Marlow withheld from Kurtz's bride-to-be. Or missing like the letter in reply to an offer sent by the Moravians to Rebekah when she was old and depleted, a wraith sheltering herself under Fort Christiansborg's walls. An offer of free passage across the sea to the Americas and Europe, to her two dead daughters, one dead husband buried there. The Moravians' gift like a long canoe offering to row R across the slaveroad. A gift you declined, R, choosing instead to remain in Africa, remain what all of us are: wanderers, wandering.

Letters and stories and daughters missing. LGS and R share many, many missing things. Yes/No. Where are they now.

Those commonalities. Those *wounds* might be a more incisive word for losses a slaveroad inflicts. You, LGS and R, bound together in a sort of sisterhood as I feel bound almost in brotherhood with WHS.

I am more fortunate than R. I have a daughter alive. She resides and works in the same city I do. Seeing her no problem. Though I seldom do. Often worry about her. Watch my daughter watch her mother, my ex-wife from whom I have been divorced thirty years, watch my daughter watch her mother's heart sinking because her mother could not convince the world her son's heart, my daughter's younger brother's heart, my son's heart, was good, a good-boy heart in a good good boy, but her mother, my former wife, couldn't persuade the ones holding him in prison for life to let him go, so her mother's heart breaking, mind failing in the stink of her Maine bedroom, twist of bedclothes, string of body, her mother unforgiving, not talking much, not much left in the last straw of a mother's body and mother's mind for a daughter to watch except her mother's heart breaking, not much mother to find or grieve after my daughter's rescue drive alone at night on I-95, etc., north from NYC to the woods, the lake, the fouled rumple of isolated house with its tiny dock at the end of a path she had walked down many mornings with her mother, each wrapped tight in bathrobe or towel against dawn chill even in

July, August, walked out the rear door to the lake and then she was a naked little girl beside her naked mother shivering, toweling off, both of them hopping, shivering, a hundred yards from the house, on the dock they reached by a path through trees and thick undergrowth, and one morning her mother's hand had touched my daughter's bare shoulder and stilled her shaking, stopped her breath, quieted her innards, her bones, limbs, all of her instantly still as frigid dawn light still above white mist hovering still above stillness of the lake, a mother's touch speaking without uttering a sound, that mother's hand, whose pale fingers had spoken to her long before she had words to remember anything by, before learning words for *quiet, noise, daughter, brother*, before words for *gripping a steering wheel*, during a drive to Maine to save her mother, before words for things inside herself she could not speak yet surely understood, things touching like her mother's touch, a vast wordless sea, a quiet and calm and chaos shifting, shifting, shifting, one thing never only one thing very long before it becomes another and another and barely manageable almost like icy plunges when they *dip*, her mother's word for it, *dipping* what they do together at dawn, Maine summer after Maine summer printing indelible and welcome and easy, the bitter chill of a dip snatching my daughter's breath away so quick, so easy and relentless, it's not even her then, her and not her in the frigid lake water, she's gone elsewhere, absolutely still, waiting for her mother's words to save her from freezing, drowning, listening for words unspoken, words enwrapped perhaps in a silent touch so you must always first look into your mother's eyes to be sure or to guess or to discover or to wonder what a touch says, the touch demanding all of your attention, all of you dripping, shuddering, hungry for whatever a touch means, oh daughter, oh dear, dear girl . . .

And low and behold one morning on the Maine dock, your mother touches you and your eyes vault up and you see in your mother's eyes a moose and baby moose gliding not more than twenty yards away, passing by too impossibly close, you think your mother must be dreaming the immense, weird profile of towering moose body silently treading, the long long thread legs, knobby knees and ankles, the child moose body a small mirror beside it, both creatures silent as shadows as they silently slip silently closer and farther away, mom moose in charge, moving delicate and serene through woods thick and tangled as dark *mess* of hair, her mother calls it, *mess* when combing or brushing or just fingers messing or unmaking that nappy, dark mess on top your head or she just pats it, plays with it, and you never know, you can only guess what's coming next, but feel it sometimes true as guesses truly feel sometimes. Like that morning on the dock beside the lake, guessing what your mother's seeing, what she means when she touches your shoulder, what you see in her eyes and feel down to your toes, a stillness seizing you like the lake's cold fist grabs and dips you under till you lance up, splash out, sputtering, shocked, trembling, not quite frozen to death again, as you hustle your little butt double-time up a ramp of wide planks cut from Maine pine trees, trees through which a mother moose and baby moose quiet beyond quiet are passing, *shhhhhh*, touch says as you stand beside your mother on the dock, and your eyes follow hers, watching as she watches, and don't dare make a sound, eyes watching her mother's heart breaking.

Stories, children, photos gone missing.

I awaken in the midst of my missing grown-up grandchild's nightmare. I am with my son's screaming, flailing daughter who's strapped on a conveyor belt programmed to impel a captive through utter, stinging darkness to reach one gender or another, a he or a she, a she or a he, and he isn't, she isn't, but the belt with its own iron will determines who he must be or she or they must be, whatever, wherever, here or there, according to the belt's wisdom. The belt imitates time. Imitates life's fatal speed and fatal destinations. Ignores my grandchild's thrashing, the struggle to figure out why and how. The belt imposes answers that a force beyond anybody's control, it seems, has already locked in place. *Help me, help me*, I hear my grandchild calling. Hear him, hear her, hear them imploring. My own heart breaking because I'm helpless to stop the belt's progress. Its irrevocable conclusions. You are this or that. You are either/or. So just shut up. You and she and he and they and her and him, all of you, the belt commands, just shut the fuck up. Grin. Enjoy the ride.

Lucy Gantt, college grad, after waiting ten years for an invitation, abandons a loving mother, a teaching job in Florida, to marry S and labor diligently beside him at Luebo mission on the Congo River. After two infant daughters die of African fevers, she's desperate to save the life of a third, and returns with her newborn baby to America, stays there until she believes her child healthy and safe, then, rather than risk her daughter's life by exposing her again to the killing rigors of a tropical climate, with great regret LGS leaves her little girl behind to be raised by an aging grandmother, and at the risk of her own life, LGS rejoins her husband at Luebo, only to discover from one of the African women or girls, probably a student befriended in the mission school where LGS teaches English and pupils instruct her in Bakete and a creole they call Kru-boy—in one of those exchanges that are unpredictable, improvised mixes of words from many languages and local tribal dialects and a speaker's idiosyncratic personal tics, in other words in the typical mode of people conversing in any international, polyglot hub of commerce, in such an exchange Lucy discovers that while she was away, her beloved husband, S, was not faithful, not too busy with God's work to neglect the devil entirely, slipping off at night to this or that very welcoming wench, and his seed Shepete birthed by one of the loose women, people say, and me, I dunno know so, so maybe yes maybe no he bery bery bery busy round here sho-nuff bery but me no know no talky no not my busy-ness, Missy, lady m'sahib, but better beware all me be saying beware, Missy, 'cause you good lady nice lady all-time nice thankee you please, Missy, and Lucy Gantt Sheppard nods back speechless, stands there nodding, clean out of words and too much a Christian to scream in the girl's lying black nigger face, No . . . not true, it is not true, not true, how dare you say what you just said when it's not true, and you know it's not, but I won't scream at you, not cuss out a child of God, God's daughter like my two lost babies, all children His children, even this African girl though she speaks evil, untrue words, speaks ugly, how do you dare speak such ugly things with God's all-seeing eye watching you, child, Him hearing every word and every untrue word hurts me, hurts Him, but great Almighty God I will not curse her, just let me breathe, please, allow me please a deep breath, Lord, a half-a-sob and I will swallow all the rest inside me and take me to my bed, lay myself down next to my poor, faraway baby's empty crib, lay myself down in that marriage bed they say S fouled while I traveled cross an ocean to save a daughter he called his darling, precious girl, my tiny girl I didn't dare bring back here, no no not for his sake, his name, no S to love and cherish, but my daughter alive, thank God and thank His mercy, my girl not dying here with me here beside her, seeing her die no no, they said, back home across the water they said don't you dare go back, Lucy, you don't have to go, Lucy, neither one of you, both y'all stay here, let it go, let Sheppard do as he must do according to his lights and conscience but don't sacrifice one more sweet God's child to do it with him, girl, stay here with your daughter, in America, where you belong, Lucy, let Sheppard go and Godspeed, let Sheppard and God tend them heathen souls,

Lucy, your place here, don't go back, and I say yes, yes my little girl surely stays here with you all, but I got to go, I love and trust God, love and trust S, please, please, I am only breath and bone, but when the wench finished her speech no bone left and all the breath of me seeps out in one unhappy sigh as wide, as wild as this wide, wild, mournful, sad, churning river we sleep beside, dying here beside this long long river carrying so much pain and blood you can't help listening some nights to how persistently it lashes and scrapes and scars and gouges the riverbank flying past and thank goodness no filthy water no, no flood, no dark wet weight, nothing to lift when I rise up from this jerry-rigged-like-everything-else-around-here packing-crate desk supposed to be a teacher's desk and nothing to it, to me as I float away, rise and shimmer away, Lord, let me reach out and touch my faraway child and then I will breathe air again for her sake, breathe in once and then let it go, let it all go, all my breath go, thankful, in Jesus' name, I did not bloody this child-woman's African face, thankful I did not rip it with my talons, her black skin, black grinning evil words, and how do I know it wasn't her own self she was telling on and laughing inside the whole time she's up in my face, her black face so serious and sad, God help me, take me home to my babies, etc. etc., oh Lord what a fool risking everything, giving S everything and now Jesus save me . . . etc. . . . etc. . . . her story goes.

S remains away in a long canoe downriver to buy supplies for the mission from the Belgians, and Lucy's story continues the day after she hears the African girl's words. Three days may be all that's left of her time alone, she thinks, or perhaps more, much, much more time alone if rapids or cannibals swallow Sheppard's dog-sorry ass, only three days left for her to rage and rectify, to recompose herself, to destroy every single remnant reminding her of S's presence, of love, three days to smash and trash so that when S comes back he will stand stupefied in the doorway, shocked, appalled by damage she has achieved during his absence, see with his own two lying eyes everything he prizes, his possessions that prop up his vanity, his courage and strength and sense of superiority, singularity, divine calling, all strewn about the household in grizzly chunks, cinders, clumps, and nappy shambles littering bamboo mats like Samson's proud hair after Delilah's scissors, and LGS prays, forgive me, Jesus, and yes, begs her sweet savior if he pleases may the sight blind S just exactly at the moment he views it, witnesses atrocious damage her long absence from his heart has wrought upon the orderly interior of a good wife, helpmate, loving mother, and Christian.

Behold, S. Look, lookee here, S. Look inside the walls of this shabby dwelling, these walls of my flesh, you dirty, defiling, evil man, and her story (his) continues about a terrible, ungrateful, sneaky, conniving S, and what a shame S is before God and man, fucking everything he can get his nasty fingers on, girl, woman, goat, chicken, any living, breathing creature around here, a snake or these wheezing, sweating, mincing, simpering, nasty pastors and priests and parsons, wouldn't they jump at the chance, white, black, brown, old, young, Christian, cannibal, a hippopotamus, octopus, why not anything, everything after she has left here and gone begging good God to spare her baby and S goes wild with lust, chasing anything moving, her him it them that, that dead boy, too, she bets when she snatches up the albums, sees many pictures of that pretty dead boy and she bets yes, bets him, too, yes, yes, his pale face among photos of bare-breasted, long-breasted African women, why not a boy lover, too, why not, thinking why in the hell not as she rips out and destroys every single image she finds of that smiling, smirking, cutie-pie little mama's white boy in the woods saving nigger souls, screwing niggers, by God it just might be, could be true, sweet boy sweet on her sweet S and S, her once-upon-a-time sweet S, her twisted S, sweet on Lapsley, Lapsley sweet on him every day God sent, every day they sneaked away and twisted up to make unnatural love to each other. LGS rips out, tears up, spits on, burns every picture of

L and S together, of Lapsley solo in books of photos or stuck on the walls of what was supposed to be her home and never will be again. When she finishes her story, nobody, nobody home ever again.

Slaveroad. Slaveroad, I say to the Uber driver. Slaveroad, please. And hurry, please. I need to go there and then get back home. Hurry.

GLORY

Glory days surround William Henry Sheppard, swirl past him, and anyone looking at him—if they spoke his language and acquainted with the word—would think *beatific* if they observed the flicker of a smile lighting up S's face an instant before he blinks. S blinks. Glory gone. He is sitting up in a rocker or bed, he's not sure which, and tries to open his eyes and not sure if his eyes open or closed while he searches for legs, dull weight of legs, remembering them, murmuring to himself, taking inventory—hand, arms, neck, back, head, eyes, two legs either stretched out flat, leaden, sweaty under bedding, or his knees bent, butt and back folded into the rocker's hard wooden seat, slippered feet on the floor, yes, no, no, yes, inventory of numb, dumb body parts forgetting him absolutely as sometimes he's able to ignore them, these stranger's body parts he summons now, recalling parts of himself, parts of this room he occupies, room he scans before he's sure his eyes open or not. Then fear. Rush to be somewhere else. Not gone. Not nowhere. Not suddenly. Dully. No one. Patience, S thinks. No rush. Lucy's voice sooner or later will open a safe rabbit hole in this silence.

He is sitting up in bed. Tea in a cup, cup on saucer, saucer on table at head of bed. Tea hot or cold. Dozed off. Hot. Blow on hot tea with his breath, careful it's very hot, you be careful now, S. Let it cool some, you hear me, Lucy had said, and tea still warm on his lips now first sip of tea after blowing, blowing softly, lips puckered is if he's fixing to kiss tea.

Lucy brought tea on a tray. Set tea down, teacup on saucer on the busy bedside night table she tidies a bit before she goes. Hot sip. Cold now. Tea set down five, ten minutes ago. Hours, maybe days ago. How long to cool. How long to happen. To change to cold. How do you know. Patience, S. Never rush. Do not count after you lock on a hippo. Patience. No counting—it's your time, all of it—take your time, draw a bead, hold steady, wait patiently, even though the beast slips underwater, wait until it rises again, wait all the seconds, minutes, years of your life. Do not count them. Do not be afraid of losing them, losing time as you level the barrel, breathe, breathe, wait to see fat, furrowed hippo brow again in your rifle's sights, keep the line straight, centered, a tight string like when line connects to a fish and you jerk, no, do not jerk, you squeeze slowly, slowly, patience, S, take your time. *Ka-pow*, and the shot-dead hippo gently sinks from view, but he, Mr. Hippo, he be back, Africans say, back maybe hour, maybe more, maybe less. Mr. Hippo you caught between the eyes or up one gaping nostril wider than a Sunday-paper funny-page Negro's nose-hole, straight up to tiny brain, then yum yum hippo meat cooking later, if you wait.

Mr. Hippo pops up, belly first, wobbles upside down in muddy current and we will swim to it, knives, spears hook it, drag it out, butcher it, meat for days, they sing and dance, clapping, patting your back, S. They yodel your name, Sheppard . . . Sheppard, great hunter, crack shot, him never miss, deadly like god lightning bolt and they love you, love you, love the sunken hippo, wait for him, S, him surely return, break water like monkey screech break bush silence, Massa Sheppard, please wait, wait please, Massa Sheppard, sir, and Mr. Hippo float belly-up, floating fresh meat ready to eat raw or roast in fire after the boys fish him out.

If you are patient, S, and wait two minutes, two hours, two years, who knows. Who knows why or when African fever comes and goes. You burn. Chilled. Melt. Afloat. Shuddering, trembling, you blow on hot tea to make it cold, blow on cold hands to make them warm, hot cold hot cold hot swimming in your own terrible wetness and you never forget fever will return even as fever breaks. The helpful Baptists at Matadi Station warned Mr. Lapsley and warned you, Mr. Lapsley's colored boy, S, about the dreaded, deadly fevers, as if you both didn't already know, already fear fever, dream fever dreams before you landed in Africa, as if the information, gossip, tips, science, words the practical Baptist missionaries dispensed—three types: [1] remittent, [2] intermittent, [3] bilious hematuria—as if their words a prescription, a cure. Like five grains of calomel, five grains of jalap tea, fifty grains of quinine, those powders, charms you had packed, of course, though they are no cure either, you learned, just buying time, fever perhaps will diminish, hide awhile before it resurfaces worse, fever never ending, you learned, the hulking, skulking, raging fever beast crosses an ocean, never losing your scent, its ravenous hunger for your stinking sweat, chills, hot flashes, shivering meat; no, no, S, it won't go away, it waits and you suffer the waiting and suffer worse when it springs up, tops you, and you drop down on your knees, crushed, legs totally giving out, they melt under you, you suffer no legs and collapse in bed until in due time, given God's mercy and grace, you sit up again, fever wanes it seems until it pounces again, finds you here, now, in this Kentucky thousands of miles, years away on a slaveroad from a mosquito-breeding, pestilence-breeding Congo River, no cure for fever, no cure for color or darkness or light or lies, no cure in Latin names given to sickness or pain or suffering, names the missionaries stick in you like pins, knives, spears, only a matter of time between one killing seizure and the next, how long how long, do not ask S do not count S wait S squeeze, draw your deadly bead on the wrinkled brow, on little piggy pop eyes, long whisker-stubbled snout, Negroid tunneled like yours.

You wait for Lucy's voice, Sheppard . . . Sheppard, are you okay, Mr. Sheppard. Him will pop up, the cannibals promise, Mr. Hippo my righteous bullets hunt to feed them . . . *ka-pow, pow, pow*. Floating in waters unbroken silence the dead hippo floats they say. Life floats, too. They say.

Sheppard remembers small splotches of light floating, miscellaneous patterns of splotches without a pattern in silent shadows where play of light and dark a sort of quiet, quiet, not quite audible music during walks when he used to walk and walk or now ghost walks on rumors of legs, ghost feet walking a backcountry road with tall trees growing beside it and thick branches overhanging, deep shadows and quiet broken by sun's brightness that prints in ink black, many, many, many intricate layers of backlit leaves in air and upon gray tar of a roadway.

But not exactly quiet, deeper silence than quietness, more complicated, nearly absolute darkness except those scattered blots shivers echoes ghosts streaks splatters webs blinks of light he walks through, steps on, listens to.

On some long stretches of country road no trees provide cover, only bushes, brambles, tangles of greenery, nothing taller than him along a burning-hot Kentucky road. No shade, no disks, spills, measures, splashes of light tremble, floating here and there, yet S still hears if he's patient, hears despite withering heat and brightness, when he lets his legs remember ambling, he remembers music that beckoned like cool, sparkling leaf-shadows once upon a time while he, while we walk, walking, walking, eyes open now, S is sure his eyes are open. No hurry. Fever comes, goes forever.

You must have figured out by now if you are still listening to me, if you are still paying attention to these words recovering, discovering, and sampling stories about S, by S and by others, me rearranging, subtracting, adding bit after bit, writing words, paragraphs, pages, passages, story after story I wrote once and maybe even once published, but rewritten now, part of this old/new S story, autobiography, slaveroad story—you should have guessed by now that the point is, I don't really want it to stop. I want to paddle downstream, upstream, and back and down and up and more and more, searching, seeking a place of refuge, of welcome where I can start to construct more story. Like S in his memoir, like anybody spinning threads of story, of fiction to protect, replace, rehearse, conceal, or repeat what I cannot forget.

MY STORY

It's about 7:30 p.m. here. The sun high in the sky and it will stay up there at least another couple hours before it descends. Early July and the sky remains very light very late at night here in Brittany, and I get up from my writing table on the deck to take down clothes hanging in the backyard because even if sky bright, dew begins to fall or rise or thicken or do whatever dew does in Brittany predictably about 7:30 p.m. these long summer days, and clothes dried on the line will get soaked again if you don't take them indoors, so I will take my stuff down as I used to take down our stuff, hers and mine, before the lies, before betrayals, her clothes always gathered first from the line because they make me feel her present, no matter where in the house or town or world she might be, and I treated her clothes differently than mine, carefully squeezing clothespins open, taking down and folding her stuff piece by piece, stacking it in its own neat pile on a wicker chair beside a large wicker hamper set on the grass under the clothesline, then the rest of the laundry grabbed, piled or tossed into the hamper, and last, the neat stack of her things placed on top.

When I finish taking down my things today, I will go back to the round writing table and chair on the deck, to the story I had looked up from to see a washer load of laundry flapping in a seven thirty Brittany breeze. A big, cloudless sky will still be up there, and on a plate next to my wineglass a green scrap left over from a tomato I'd eaten, a little bowl of grape tomatoes, slices of saucisson my aperitif, and I pick up the detached green whatever from my plate to examine it closer and it was/is exquisite, a small, wilting five-pointed star silhouetted when I raised and dangled it by the tiny green tip of one point against blue sky, and believe me, the word for it, *exquisite*, though I have no words to tell how unexpected and unique that particular dying piece of vegetable matter, how delicate, how unerringly complete, no words to tell its story, but I see it, hear it, a stem and leaves approximately a quarter inch in length when centered in my palm, a green root or handle or hand, you could call it, that once fastened a grape tomato to a vine, but no words for how perfectly shaped, elegant, exquisite it is, so I will shut up. My clean laundry stuffed in the hamper, mostly dry, ready to be put away later. Her presence and her absence, and where oh where now, and I will go back to my writing table, wine, aperitif, no words to tell the story, and even if I found some, they would not bring my *Lucy* back any sooner.

The sky darkens, ignoring a forecast of sunny day after sunny day along Brittany's coast. No sky visible, no stars perforate a lid of blackness tonight, and sheets, sheets, sheets of rain are falling, drowning me in my garden where I sit and weep, and rain washes away my tears, my tears wash away rain. Oh, what a night, the Dells sang. And what peace in the morning.

NTOMANJELA

William Henry Sheppard became a renowned storyteller during his popular lecture tours in America. "A Girl Who Ate Her Mother" may be S's favorite African story. Recorded in *Presbyterian Pioneers*, told and retold countless times on the lecture circuit, published by him once as a children's book. Why his favorite, if in fact it is. The answer to that why is as inaccessible to me as the names of the owners of those teeth in a dentist's box that fascinated S when he was a boy. But anyway here is one more retelling (mine) of S's favorite story:

Ntomanjela . . . Ntomanjela . . . One afternoon I returned from a trip south to buy supplies and recruit souls, and Mr. Lapsley told me that while I was away, he had heard someone calling him, one of his friends using Mr. L's Bekete name, Ntomanjela, the name meaning "pathfinder" because Africans believed Mr. L had found the way into their country, their homes, language, and hearts. Turns out Mr. L's friend had come round to share with Ntomanjela a story he'd heard about a cannibal leading captives to market. A woman slave's feet too swollen to take another step and she dropped down beside the trail and the cannibals camped there and ate her and caused the woman's young daughter to eat of her also.

Of course, Sheppard, I was terrified by the tale, Mr. L said, and then he told me that when he learned the band of slavers remained nearby, he felt he must go and demand they cease such hideous acts. l intended to demand gently, Mr. L said, despite his outrage, his rage, and I believe he probably did speak gently, since gentle always how Mr. L dealt with people, and also, being no fool, he feared cannibals.

The chief of the party, though somewhat annoyed by a white man's unexpected appearance at a juncture on the trail it was the cannibals' custom to use, consented to speak with Mr. L. Told him that he had followed the usual procedure and that it also made perfect sense. If too weak to march, a slave becomes a burden for others. Daughter hungry, alive, and valuable merchandise. Why should she not be fed.

Mr. L said he implored the cannibal chief to leave the unfortunate orphan behind. The chief said he would exchange the girl for a goat. Mr. L offered instead a bolt of foreign cloth and a bargain was struck. A mission woman took the naked child to the river, washed and clothed her. Ntombi will be a student in our schoolhouse, Mr. L said to me, and God willing, she will thrive.

Ntombi became Mr. L's favorite. He kept her especially close about him for the final ten, eleven months left him on this earth. And from her very first days in the mission, quite predictably difficult days for her, she favored Mr. L with her trust, her smile. His hands, embraces, smiles the only ones she did not ignore, resist, fight, hiss at, or run away from screaming. She loved Mr. L immediately as we all do. Ntombi shy, but on occasion boldly affectionate, Mr. L confided once to me. If he wasn't wary, she would sneak into his bed, he said, and curl up next to him until he awakened in the morning.

Ntombi became Ntomanjela's quiet shadow. Serving him, nursing him, imitating him. At ease at last, and a favorite too, in the flock of mission women, suffering women that Mr. L and I both worried about because they were neither exactly fish nor fowl, not property, not protected by chiefs or family males, thus misfits, our mission's crew of fearful, dependent women, a congregation of discontented souls, always hungry, begging for more, semipermanent residents or nomads passing through, our female wards, with some of whom I admit I expressed myself most freely, in a manner that gentle, shy Mr. L never would or could, and he admonished me saying he feared that my attentions to the women endangered my soul, souls of the women, and how right he was about Adam's weakness, right about them, those clamorous women, dusky Eves, innocent, shy, curious, wild in this untamable, dark garden, women forever beseeching, squabbling amongst themselves, women who obediently sang hymns, obediently chanted prayers we taught them, our pack of pagans who would worship a python or lie down with one if they believed they'd be rewarded with a meal or shelter.

In Mr. L's eyes Ntombi a quiet, pious jewel among our female charges. A blessed daughter, little mother, helpmate.

Ntombi crushed, I'm certain, when Ntomanjela did not return on the government steamer from Stanley Pool. Ntombi mourns him today, no doubt, if she is still alive. No telling what they might have become to one another. But that's another story.

TEA

Lucy Gantt Sheppard brings the glass teapot into a room too full of furniture to breathe. A woman not small, not large, not exactly shrunken, but clearly not the woman she once was. Old but substantial as each piece of polished furniture, furniture oversized for the room's modest dimensions, furniture whose every flat surface, whose every shelf visible through spotless glass is loaded with knickknacks, photos in ornate frames, painted crockery, vases; LGS an old woman crowded, competing for air with all the stuff she's accumulated to surround herself—antiques, relics, African masks, an imposingly massive oak sideboard, miniature figurines of porcelain, ivory, carved wood—a room full of last things belonging to her that she no doubt cares for meticulously, years of gathering, dusting, shining, arranging, rearranging, attending these inanimate objects dying with her in this old house, this overburdened space paid for dearly and dearly owned, this museum of purchases and prosperity perfectly preserved as her undulled eyes that remain curious and restless, young, a smile that's young, too, despite papery, freckled skin, wrinkles, white wisps of hair escaping edges of a kerchief tied to conceal bare spots and purple veins I picture atop a pale skull, a perfect housekeeper perfectly prepared to let the manner she cares for this room, into which she invites me for a cup of tea, introduce her, display her, tell her story if I or any other visitor desires to hear it, and whether anyone asks for a story or not, whether she survives the room or not, whether it survives her, the room narrates who she is, was, these objects, her ancient possessions, each with its own history and destiny, speak for her while I sit and watch her pour hot water over tea bags into two teacups.

Why me, a question she addresses as much to herself as to me. Or addresses to no one in particular, just a way of ending an awkward silence opening, then expanding between us, a pause after cups filled, and she hesitates, handle of glass teapot gripped in one fist, pot holder in her other hand ready to steady the pot, as if she's lost track of what she must do next to complete a simple action she intends. As if adrift, unable momentarily to remember or forget until she asks *why me*, to end a silence suddenly become too long, too complicated for either of us, total strangers before this meeting, to ignore or negotiate. A brimful, wary silence inconsistent with polite exchanges. Silence a vast emptiness calling attention to itself, consuming more than its proper share of the room's sparse air.

On the round mahogany table a rooster-shaped metal trivet atop a circular mat finally accepts the teapot. Before she vanishes again, my host, this Lucy Gantt Sheppard I found after years of searching, seats herself on a chair matching mine, matching five others matching the table. Her posture perfect, back straight, shoulders squared, no droop to her chin. She is substantial again, not dead, as I'd begun to assume after failing to discover any trace of her in public records after her husband's death in 1927. Lucy Gantt Sheppard not small, even though cut in half by the tabletop's black, shining immensity separating us in this room of a house on East Breckinridge Street, Louisville, KY, a room, a house, street, neighborhood all of which have seen better days, and worse too, I heard in her voice, why *me*, before she sat down, before she shakes her head slowly and sighs, All that time . . . all that long, long time . . .

Not the kind of day I would have chosen for a Martin Luther King birthday party. But happy to celebrate King, happy to join marchers around Philadelphia's City Hall. I will participate to honor him, the man he might have continued to struggle to be if his life, his time on earth, had not been stolen. Way past the point now, of course, for marches, protests—Martin day . . . George day . . . who you saying . . . what's his last name . . . George . . . that murdered guy . . . name starts with *F* . . . Foreman . . . huh-uh . . . Floyd . . . Floyd . . . George Floyd—George Foreman's the boxer—a crazy dude—too many punches to the head, man, named all his sons George, didn't he—like what the fuck's the difference, anyway—just names—King lost, and another and another shot dead in the streets, and protesting, marching, speeches won't bring them back nor stop the next one from being killed.

Way past the point now of needing responses, protests futile as I was sure the King Day march would be. Futile as trying to stay warm outdoors on an icy, snow-flogged day at the end of January. Futile as pretending anything less than total erasure and beginning again from scratch will change this town, its citizens, my people, my country. But I can't give up on symbols yet. A writer, after all. *Futility, hope.* Aren't they more than words, symbols. Who can say, let alone know, what's coming next.

No invitation to the mayor's reception. Hope I don't sound bitter. I am not. Quite the contrary. Grateful, rather, on Martin Luther King Day, invitation or no invitation, to get quickly out of bitter cold, into a heated room furnished with hot beverages, an assortment of sweet rolls and donuts, and however I managed to wind up there—rumor of a mayor's reception circulating through participants in the march, heads-up from an old acquaintance, or following a prosperous-looking group that appeared to know where they were headed and in a hurry and confident they would arrive and be cared for—I felt I belonged. Appreciated the warm cup of tea a young woman behind a long table draped by a white cloth poured for me. A pleasure to blend in unobtrusively. No fanfare, no profuse exchanges of greetings, hugs, smiles, Ooh-La-La kisses on both cheeks of ladies, my old trademark, confirming my sophistication, my distinguished reputation not only at home but abroad. Thankful in this familiar setting where once I'd wasted far too much time, far too many words, thankful that no bullshit required today. Just me warming up, my tea cooling.

When I noticed Sheppard he was standing near the mayor, who was beside someone in a wheelchair. The shock of white hair is what drew my eyes to fasten on Sheppard. Anonymous white cusp of hair, then Sheppard. Unmistakably him. William Henry Sheppard. Too much space intervened between us to calculate precisely how much his face had aged. But white hair signifies ancient to me. Death just around the corner. Keep my few short hairs cropped quite close, nipped in the bud to avoid telltale white blooming of age in my sideburns or white sprinkling the corona circling half my skull just above and behind my ears if I let hair grow longer than half a quarter inch. White hair I often admire on other people's heads but dread on mine, white caught my eye across the ballroom, a head covered by hair white as graying snow shoveled and banked along city streets to clear a path for the Martin Luther King march.

I held my casual glance for an extra moment, hoping no one noticed, hoping to assure myself that indeed it was our tall Mr. Mayor next to a brown man in a wheelchair, and yes, near the mayor, Sheppard's face wearing an ancient person's hair. Sheppard not forgotten despite my not seeing him for many years, then wondering how long it could've been since I had last encountered Sheppard. Not recently, but not a hundred years ago either. Huh-uh, no, impossible it's been that long, I was thinking, trying to remember how long until I realized I was staring again and abruptly stopped studying him, looked away. Impossible, I couldn't help myself from thinking, because if S had aged so much, turned so white in the interval since our last meeting, then certainly I, too, must have altered as drastically. Perhaps dead like him.

Whether or not S's face an unflattering mirror, whether or not I would discover in his face more undeniable bad news, I had no desire to approach him and confront whatever his white hair, his eyes greeting mine might reflect. Fact that S, my elder by many, many dozens of years, did not allay my panic. *Panic* the precise word. Turned on my heels in a panic, fled through a crowd grown much thicker now after word of free drinks, free food had leaked out, me careful not to step on a blue ribbon lying on the floor, ribbon once stretched between two waist-high brass stanchions to barricade space between the ballroom's open double doors where I entered. Staff long gone now who had been tending the ribbon and checking names earlier as I nonchalantly sauntered in, veteran me knowing better than to stop, attaching myself instead to whatever notable or notables I understood would not hesitate, not offer their names, and no attendant would dare ask.

Do I inhabit a transparent globe of immeasurable dimensions, glass, sealed, no exits or entrances fathomable to me. An all-encompassing singularity of consciousness, of terror I cannot escape.

Sheppard's white shock of hair not as white of course as it first appeared. Color less a matter of actual color than associations color triggers. And *shock* not a very accurate word to describe what covers

S's head. Sprinkles. *Sprinkles* not the perfect word either, but better. Like you might say *white* is how a street, a roof, a lawn looks after snow sprinkles it. Sprinkle, sprinkle, little hairs. Sheppard's snowy hair a detail I might easily have missed or ignored when I scanned City Hall's so-called ballroom from my chosen corner. Difference of his hair barely stopping my gaze. White color or lack of color a minor note within dull theme and variations of brown, gray, occasionally black or blond, but predominately blue-haired guests the mayor had invited.

White hair about more than color. Sometimes while I'm shaving, if I happen to spot a white hair in a nostril, I have to stop immediately, pick or snatch or scissor it out. A hair whiter, more urgent than it actually is, and that's how I reacted to a whitish head I had noticed in the reception crowd. Probably a tall mayor leaning down and talking to a brown man in a wheelchair equally responsible for arresting my gaze, revealing ancient Sheppard.

I avoided William Henry Sheppard on Martin Luther King Day. Seeing him from a distance sufficed, I believed. Believed it would be wise just to let him go. If I didn't acknowledge Sheppard's presence, maybe he wasn't really there. He would disappear.

More than ironic that Sheppard had popped up, with his white shock or white sprinkles, on the January day of a march and reception for King, a day circled in red on our nation's calendar of forget-me-not commemorations. The sort of special day William Henry Sheppard deserved. I had written not long before to an old friend, editor of an influential journal, describing WHS as more or less forgotten by the American public, a man I had recently discovered purely by accident whose story fascinated me enough that I immediately had begun to research his career. My letter was an attempt to convince my editor/buddy to initiate in his prestigious journal a campaign for a WHS Day to honor the unique achievements of an extraordinary human being who absolutely deserved more national recognition. Took a while for the journal editor to respond, a whole lot longer than I expected, given our long acquaintanceship and what I had assumed was mutual respect. Didn't S's unique story speak for itself. WHS a missing link. S connecting America and Africa in a rather startling fashion seldom acknowledged, seldom explored by traditional historians, thus unsuspected, virtually unknown territory for ordinary citizens.

Got my old running buddy on the phone, finally, and he pleaded, C'mon, man. You of all people must know this S dude poison. Me and a couple staff folks pretty hip to him, but soon as I mentioned your idea, the ones even a little bit aware of WHS rolled their eyes, started to wag their heads, no, no, not one of my people even sort of agrees with you. Yeah, yeah, S something else, an unusual brother, especially back in those times, those evil days. A sure enough cooking brother. Anybody got to be impressed by him. The dude way out there back then, but the baggage, his baggage, you know what I'm talking about, man. Presbyterians snatched his ass out the Congo. Boy lucky they didn't lynch him when they got him back home. Lucky they only rusticated his randy behind and didn't flat out defrock him. Course we both know he isn't first colored preacher fucking colored church ladies, but shit, Sheppard steady humping African honeys and making babies over there. What's worse, brother let his wife and them cracker missionaries catch him red-handed. Least one little son named after Sheppard crawling around the Congo compound. No no no. Almost had no MLK Day behind shit like that, bro, so can't help you with this project, my friend. No way, José. Still, tell the truth, I dig the cat just like you do. But best forget about it, man. Leave it alone. Sheppard fucked up big. Women around here would burn me at the stake and my little raggedy magazine too, we start agitating for some kind of WHS Day.

I tried but failed to convince the editor I had no desire to promote a WHS story that excluded or slighted LGS or disparaged women in general. Believe you, my man, he said, but good intentions not worth shit these trifling days.

Not easy for me, Lucy Gantt Sheppard says, sitting up board straight, eyes fixed on mine across the dark expanse of dining room table. And if you are familiar, sir, she continues, even a tiny bit familiar with my history, and you must be some, because you found me, didn't you, and here we sit in my home and you're going to ask whatever you need to ask, but anyway, I will start by saying, even though I'm guessing you may already know more than enough about Lucy Gantt Sheppard, that no matter what else you found written about me or folks have whispered in your ear, I need to add this. It's not easy for me even now, after all the long, long years, to go back to Congo. Even going back only in my own mind.

Congo hurt me once. And still hurts. More than words can say. Other people's words or my words, if I can make myself say them. Person like you, a man as you are, and being a man a blessing for you, you ought to be grateful, I believe, but you cannot even start to imagine how hard it was back in those days for a person like me in Africa. A woman, a mother, a wife, a teacher, a lover. Hard enough anytime, anyplace to be those things, do those things. To do what others expect of me. What I expect and demand from myself. All that, and color, which I have not even mentioned.

Africa. Congo. Beautiful sometimes. I loved how Africans spoke. Their voices reminded me of home. Taught myself an African language. Talk it still to myself. Africa a special place, Africans special people, S wrote me in his letters. Beautiful and sometimes terrible here in Africa, he wrote. Hard lives for Congo people, for him and the other missionaries. Strangely, when I read his letters, they aroused no fear of what might befall me when I joined him. The killing fevers preying on missionaries, relentless heat, poisonous snakes and insects, wild animals, bloody wars natives wage upon each other armed, financed by Belgian companies, floods, starvation, diseases cutting people down every day. All the horrors and perils of Congo Sheppard described seemed bearable, did not scare me nor warn me away. Haunted me only because life for me here or there unbearable, if S did not survive. When the letter I like to remember as a telegram arrived finally, telling me, Lucy, please come, and not exactly in those words, but that's all the message I recall, because nothing else in it mattered, nothing more I needed to start me packing and hurrying up, hurry up, fast as I could to join him, marry him, go off with him to another world.

And that Africa world just as beautiful, as mean, as soul-and-body crushing as what I'd heard and read. As S warned. But S did not warn me about his fickle heart, icy heart, forgetful heart, about changes he would put me through if I joined him in the Congo, and now, going back again now, thinking about him today, well, excuse me, it isn't easy. Sheppard isn't easy and I pray your soul may rest in peace, William Henry Sheppard. You done me blacker, worse than Africa ever did.

African fever took my two babies, but S took my heart. Ate it. Spit the blood in my face. Don't misunderstand me, sir, please. I don't ask "why me" because I feel my share of suffering greater than other folks' share. Just talking to myself most the time. Then a person like you at my door. Wanting me to bear witness. Bare my soul. Asking me about Sheppard. Asking about me, too, it seems. After all the years, after this long, long time, how come you think only me left to bear witness to the things you seem to want to know, sir.

Yes. Just me living in this house years and years now. But old house not empty. When people have to go they just go on and leave here. One by one they go away. Doesn't mean they are not around. Or do not return. Busy coming and going. Witnesses like me. Who else I'm supposed to talk to. Rattle round in these rooms long as

I've been rattling, you get used to bumping into people. People big as life, bright as day everywhere in this house. Love my house. All these precious Africa pieces we brought back to grace it. They can't talk exactly, but they help make this my dream home.

When I was just a tiny thing, promised my mother I'd buy her a beautiful house and we would live in it together forever and ever like happy people in those fairy tales she used to sing to me. Last few years of her life my mama, bless her soul, lived in this lovely home with me. Good years. Happy years. My promise to her come true. My children lived here too—wise, perky Wilhelmina till she left to start a home of her own, and Max, smart and a warrior like his father, but frightened of people like his father never was frightened. Max here till he left and start roaming all four corners of the globe. Sheppard here in this house when he passed in his sleep. We suffered together, good days and bad days here.

People put on earth to suffer. How else would a body know they alive. This house a woman-dream. Woman-dream a place where she can live with her people. Man-dream a throne. Nice, shiny place just for him alone to sit and pretend he a little king. Place he can puff himself up about, brag about so other men think he a big king on a big throne. No doubt about it, but I am a witness also to the truth that there's some men dream a home, some women dream a throne. Two different kinds of dream and, me, Lucy Gantt Sheppard, I just called one *man-dream*, and the other kind *woman-dream*. Woman-dream what I suffered, believed, learned all those years with S. And without him.

I imagine you prefer your days to begin briskly now, Lucy Gantt Sheppard. No lingering in bed for you. Sleep lost time for you. Why drift in the foggy labyrinth separating awake from asleep. When your eyes open (pop/snap open), you do not hesitate, do you. Put your feet on the floor, on the path towards your tasks, I bet. Your mission. You do not slip backwards, do you. Back into your dreaming. You avoid that door of no return.

Or perhaps you begin days with prayer. Prayer never ending till night comes and you fall asleep again. As I imagine Rebekah prays her way through her days. No such thing as a crisp, rushed prayer for you, is there, Lucy. Unless a person has forgotten how to pray. Forgotten that prayer is a kind of wide-awake drift towards God. Each of your prayers hovering, teasing at the edges of lasting forever, I think, Lucy. Prayer silencing you. Alone in the presence of your God. Listening. Until the silence, the mystery tells you to move, to fulfill your day. Fill it with duties, tasks, mission. Then whatever you perform, whatever you feel about all the busyness of a day become simply afterthoughts, after your morning begins alone in your God's presence. Listening. The weight of his voice heavy inside you. And light. Wings of light lifting, driving, flying you from one duty to the next. In no hurry.

HERE

I have resided here in NYC twenty-odd years now but do not feel I'm a New Yorker. Raised in Pittsburgh and not exactly a Pittsburgher either, but definitely not a New Yorker. I don't believe anyone, whether born in NYC or not, can claim this city as home. Only immigrants here, no matter how many successive generations of a person's family have resided in this city. This is a place where immigrants come seeking a home and never find it. All people you pass on the New York City streets are immigrants. The city itself an overgrown, lonely, orphaned immigrant. A city that can abide anybody's company, but refuses every person's request for refuge.

A person can't belong here because no one belongs here, is what the city keeps saying again and again and again in whatever language you speak but the city doesn't. Or says in a language you don't speak but the city does. Forget about how far you and yours go back. You are immigrants, foreigners still. No matter how much you learn, deny, improve, forget, improvise, you remain among the lost, the outsiders. Look down at the sidewalk. Peer up at the sky. Gaze all around. Behind and in front of you. You or the city disappears. Nothing of you, for you, here. Except what is not you.

Here where the city always is. Where it ends before it begins. Not you. Not home. Now you see the city, now you don't. The city goes nowhere, everywhere without you. Like a rumor of deadly disease you may not catch that kills you anyway.

Then go the fuck back to Pittsburgh, chump, a New Yorker honks at me, but since none exist, I'm only imagining a New York voice. Like I imagine a home in Pittsburgh. Like I imagine myself not an immigrant because for a lifetime I have heard words telling me precisely the name of a country, the *United States of America*, that I inhabit, and telling me who I am and where I am and where I belong in that country, words beyond familiar, words resonating bone deep so that even unspoken or unheard those words continue to identify and define me, place me, wherever I happen to be or happen to be doing, but those words no more real than anybody's claim to be a New Yorker or Pittsburgher because in this imagined country where I reside no one can be anything, not even an immigrant, unless they understand that first they are black or white, are colored or not, despite whatever else a person goes on to claim or doesn't claim to be.

Certain choices here a person is not born free to make. Here in this city we get Orders from Headquarters. Must dance the separation dance or suffer dire consequences. Or die. White and black separate as the fingers of the hand that becomes a fist that crushes you if you don't do the dance. On New York City streets, or in the slave quarters, or fiddling to entertain masters in the Big House or smiling in the mayor's seat or bent down sweating in a cotton field, you hear a song ringing in your ears. Jump about, wheel about, jump Jim Crow. And you better listen. Better enjoy while you can. Better than nothing. Better than dead, Headquarters reminds you. Honks at you—Stay in your lane, shithead.

CLOTHILDE

Sky clear the morning I look out my ninth-floor apartment bedroom window at towering ruins of city and imagine a Mars landing, imagine two of the rover's international crew my color, imagine the miracle of it all happening, a wonder especially for someone like me who can't even count from one to ten without his mind wandering and losing track, see the miraculous crew members scooting, flying, digging stuff up, riders in some sort of horse and buggy that's able to leap tall buildings in a single bound or smash obstacles aside with titanium fists, exploring, excavating a reddish surface compounded of dust, steel, sugar, concrete, and microscopic particles of a bone-like substance serving Mars as a skin like dirt serves Earth as skin, astronauts aboard a vehicle much smarter than they are if they ask it to be, a sweet chariot more accurate, more precise, more knowledgeable about where they are, where they wish to head than they will ever be, more brutal poking its perfect nose, purring lips deeper, deeper underground to partake of and understand exactly what lies beneath them and predict with astounding correctness what's coming next, sending its findings back to Earth faster than the speed of light, faster than the astronauts can download on the rover's screens, but the crew also able to talk to the machine they ride and it talks back to them when a crew member lonely, afraid, curious, sorry, hungry, or anything else, anything else anyone thinks they are or thinks they need is available, the machine promises, or soon will be, including needs of colored ones like him, if they, he, or she, happen to be colored, colored ones who a nasty rumor has it are more needy, more demanding, thus less attentive, less competent when at the controls, it's rumored in ugly messages back and forth, Earth to Mars, Mars to Earth on this very morning he's imagining them up there millions, billions of miles away up in the nothing of clear sky, there while he's here imagining them on Mars as they may imagine him, envy him, far away, the crew wondering about all that, wondering about home perhaps, but only for a split second, and maybe wondering for another split split second why data reads *CLOTHILDE*, when atoms and DNA of an ancient ship's skeleton are unearthed, a ship wandering like him from here to there and returning on the slaveroad faster than the speed of light, ship disappearing as the spacemen, spacewomen bury wonder instantaneously and concentrate absolutely on their instruments, on buzzes, drones, beeps, flashes, trills, dances of light light-years distant because they know they better, better because they know if they don't, if dey don't do no better maybe, maybe dey neber gon git home.

BOOKS

Next task, now that all the windows washed, is tossing the books littering the walls of this so-called study. Not all the books. That would hurt too much. Would be selfish, ungrateful, wasteful. Not the books' fault that he'd stopped reading them. That his mind, or what's left of it he still calls mind, erases each sentence before he begins the next. Leaving behind only scorched earth. Fragments, useless remnants like what he remembers from the boring, boring Milton class English majors at his elite university required to take, the old blind poet saying *these books which are my life, quite carry me away.* Well, no hard feelings, my old book friends, but time now to carry you away. Pack you in boxes and maybe donate you to the public library I can see out my window, down below in the island of trees and playground surrounding three sides of the twenty-story brick building I inhabit along with countless other inhabitants, a library here long before I moved into the neighborhood and will probably be here long after I'm gone, a branch of the New York City Public Library, I assume, must assume since I've never once entered its ornate stone-framed door, though I've passed by year after year because a regular consumer of paths and greenery below my ninth-floor apartment, the parklet and library just two of many pleasant amenities keeping rents high around here, and if I offered the library my boxes of books, should I, would I inquire first if any of the books I've written happen to be among the treasures stored on the local library's shelves, inquiring shyly of course, and certainly not implying I might withhold my contribution just because some bureaucrat in charge had neglected to include samples of yours truly in the local library's collection. After all, if the library had ignored me, hadn't I been at least as guilty of ignoring it the two decades or so we had shared the same turf, but very curious I'd surely be, I must admit, and probably won't be able to resist initiating a dumb exchange: Tell me, Mister (or more likely Ms.), among your copious and invaluable holdings are there any books of mine. A pity if not, I may go on to say, maybe even say a damned shame, maybe unforgivable, or careless or unlucky or whatever, particularly since yours truly—I'll introduce myself properly in a moment or two, and upon hearing my name there's a small chance, more like a minuscule chance really, that you, Miss, might have heard of me, of my many published, highly praised books, and even an infinitesimal chance that you've read one—yours truly happens in fact to reside just an elevator ride and a few steps away from your workplace's impressive front door, Miss, Sir, and that fact may more than slightly interest future literary critics and historians and perhaps even enhance the value of the gift I am contemplating bestowing upon this library, an additional incentive so to speak for your institution to accept, be pleased about, even showcase the gift in a special corner displaying the work of special authors, because my offering offers you a natural occasion for expanding your holdings, pleasing the urban audience you serve, opportunities highlighted by the special happenstance that we, you and yours truly, me, actually are and have been, it turns out, neighbors for decades, though never properly introduced nor falling in love in a city notorious for enabling strangers to become strange bedfellows or for beds to be lonely and bereft; well, hmmm, anyway, you know what I mean, and I know I'm getting way ahead of the game, writing what may come afterward for us, Miss, before I write sentences necessary to explain and precede this present moment we are sharing, this foolish exchange precisely symptomatic of the general foolishness afflicting me these days, and possibly forever, me not able to remember beyond the particular sentence at hand, remembering neither where it came from nor could be headed, so not easy for me to make any sense whatsoever of this moment, of these shelves of surplus books, mine and yours, shelves holding books in my possession that may duplicate books you possess already or not or don't wish to possess, and that's why I'm asking questions first, rather than obscurely, anonymously dumping boxes of books at night on your doorstep.

LIONS AND TAGGERS

Taggers: a name for graffiti scribblers. *Tagger* how my old aunt May pronounced the word *tiger.* Their handiwork everywhere. Artists of sorts. Basquiat once sort of one of them. One of the most ferocious. A tagger. A tiger. The best of them change what we see. Sometimes make what we see better. Often make it worse. They work hard, and mostly, I think, at night. They are often very young, I think. Wild, brave, untamable maybe as lions and tigers. Work in perilous places often. Fearless in this jungle of city. I worry about them. Believe sometimes I hear them talk:

> *When they catch us at night, they don't ask what we doing. Don't ask why we out our cages. They know we wrong. Why else we in a place at night they had told us not to be. Doing something they told us not to do. They know they must chase us or beat or capture us. Eat us, the old folks in their old down-home tales said. Kill and eat us. Which they did often, the news said.*

No questions asked. No names taken. No family alerted or warned we had been caught doing things we shouldn't. How could they tell anybody we were guilty and deserved punishment if they couldn't say what they caught us doing. They do not know what we are doing and do not ask.

Most nights working away and seem like we never finish by morning painting the world different colors. 'Cause that's what we doing, by the way, and we woulda confessed probably, if asked when cops catch us at night.

Different colors, Mr. Ossifer, sir, my homie Mumbles mumbled at the cop. Mumbles smiling when the police officer raises his big gun and shoots Mumbles in the face because Mumbles hoping a bullet might cure his speech defect. An instant miracle right there in the middle of Willy B bridge where we had just *Aghhhhhh*-ed the walkway and *R I P*-ed *Omar* on a steel blackboard's purple paint still drippy, wet under our feet.

Never wear our good shoes nights we working. Shoes leave prints. Telltale proof of shoe brand, shoe size, shoe price, our faces trapped in cameras in upscale stores. Incriminating evidence like fingerprints on somebody's eyeball you poke out trying to make a person see color better.

STARING

So here I am pushing the short story of myself to last just a bit longer. On a beach staring. As you, Rebekah, as you, Sheppard and Lucy . . . as you, and you . . . etc., etc. . . . may have found yourselves on a beach staring at the sea. Seeing a slaveroad. Or not.

I watch a woman spread her towel on the sand, pull her dress over her head, fold it, lay it beside her, unpack her lunch, settle down to eat. She sees a man who stands on a rock, in a cluster of partly submerged rocks about half a New York City block away from her. She notices or doesn't notice not far beyond the man a jumble of massive boulders and slabs of stone jutting from the foot of the steep hillside that forms a back wall shaping this cove in Brittany. When tide's up, that tall pile of huge, irregularly shaped stones becomes an obstacle course, poking up through the water and temporarily dividing one section of beach from the next, a slightly treacherous fifty-to-sixty-yard barrier you must negotiate if you wish to walk further along the shoreline, and I had climbed and picked my way many times through and over those hulking stones, tempted occasionally to mount one and gaze out over the sea, before slipping once, thirteen years ago, and tumbling like Alice through her looking glass, or plunging, one doctor surmised, not because I'd lost my footing but lost consciousness an instant during an ischemic episode and plunged, fracturing three ribs, nearly killing myself, plunged through a hole between stones, then lay dazed, groaning on a wet stone because communication between heart and brain had stalled for a second or microsecond, a potentially fatal disruption whose reoccurrence a pacemaker I wear today is supposed to prevent.

No. Not that failure, not that falling story now. Let the woman see a man standing on a rock who stares at the sea when he is not staring at her. Stare performed dramatically as if contemplating how far, how deep the water stretches, how many steps on a shimmering gold staircase to mount a throne, a gallows, how many strides atop the water—hero, warrior, prophet, lost lover—before he reaches his destiny, before the sea opens beneath his feet and he disappears or sky opens and he ascends. His stare making the drama he imagines quite palpable, making enormous distances, vast separation and yearning palpable, a stare that encroaches equally on the quiet meal the woman serves herself and her peace of mind, as if she's the one who brazenly stares, as if stolen glances not his, as if she, not he, the thief.

She's quite sure she doesn't come to the beach to pose for anyone. But also, she thinks, if a person chooses to appear in a public space, isn't that person posing for anybody who also happens to be there. Is it possible to express somehow, by the force of one's personal example, that one does not follow the general rules nor conform to usual expectations. Or possible to change the rules. Whatever rules govern play of eyes between two people, or rules that regulate a stare's aggression, a stare's subterfuge. Whose rules. Whose choices abide. Isn't her choice—her determination not only not to pose but not to be seen—a pose. While here, while palpably present on this public beach in a swimsuit, eating lunch, could she will herself invisible to the man standing on a rock, she wonders.

Chooses to ignore him. Believes her choice a kind of civilized courtesy since it costs another person nothing to reciprocate. No exchange. No connection necessary. Just like the casual, ordinary passing-by on city streets practiced daily by countless passersby. Nothing demanded, nothing offered, nothing except perhaps that other people reciprocate the courtesy. Her choice not to see nor be seen by others, a *civilized* choice, she thinks again. Then thinks, *discontents.* Smiles to herself and admits the nothing her choice desires from other people is also something.

Nothing is never exactly nothing, she thinks, even when nothing crosses a person's mind. The thought of nothing is, itself, composed of words, isn't it. Words in a person's mind live and create substance in a person's life, substance that renders one person's life different from all other people's lives. Unless absolutely nothing is what being alive is and thinking is, and nothing is truly what a life consists of. Still, she thinks, whether that dire, deflating, bottom-line truth true or not, it seems to her that almost everyone, like it or not, continues, birth to death, the effort of making something of nothing. Though nothing never becomes enough, does it. Though nothing remains nothing. A tiresome circularity, a self-fulfilling prophecy, she thinks, no matter how cleverly she games the word, nothing.

Does the man on the rock believe he's posing. For whom. Does he believe she's posing for him. Who knows. Who cares. Lunch alone on the beach, skin warmed by sun, not a pose. She loves eating alone on the beach. A book (*Rebecca's Arrival*, perhaps) all the company she requires. To read. Or not to read. Not posing. She's here because her choice is to be here. To please herself. A perk occasionally conferred by an otherwise demanding, confining job, and she understands she's lucky the building where she works is only a few minutes' walk from the sea and weather permitting when the opportunity arises she looks forward to each getaway wholeheartedly. A special treat, especially given civilization and all its discontents. Tomorrow who knows. She opens the foil wrapped round her chunk of cheese. Catches his gaze she thinks at the very instant it returns to pretending it's very busy, busy, busy elsewhere.

Should I go further with those two on the beach. Set her and him to talking on this same sand crusting the soles of my bare feet after I hump twenty minutes, up and back, up and back along a track that low tide, like an efficient, dependable, meticulous grounds crew, has cleared for the next couple hours for anyone who wishes to walk or run along this edge of the Gulf of Morbihan in Brittany. Write the woman and man here on this page while I daydream endless miles up and back, up and back along an unspeakably perfect stretch of beach.

If you reach my advanced age, you will understand what I mean when I say I am weary, weary beyond words, weary of making up a life for myself. Same old life (the story goes), dead as the lives populating the fiction I write. Write and write, on and on, day after day, pick up and start over again, picking up the pieces as if they belong to me, are mine and always have been, always will be mine, be me, though every day it seems more pieces lost than found.

As if one story or another might be right or wrong. Weariness the only reward of keeping or losing track each time.

I read a newspaper article recently about a former student of mine, and wondered if maybe I could write my student's story. Wondered if the drama of her story might enliven the dullness of mine. Wonder now if her story, and not this "woman and man staring and not staring at each other on a beach" story, is the one I need to write. Woman on the beach reminds me of my student in an oddly compelling fashion, though I can't pin down why exactly. Are the resemblances physical, metaphysical, illusory. Whatever they might be, are they worth pursuing. Isn't one reason for writing any story to ferret out and examine the reasons for writing it.

A woman eating lunch on the beach glances at a man glancing at her and I glance at them and the woman could be my student and I stare at her and she is my student and isn't and is again in countless lifetimes whirling past in less than the instant it takes me to blink. But much more happens, happening too fast, too much, and disappears, long gone before and after anyone can experience it. Gone forever probably, absolutely lost without hope of recovery *here*, but continuing to happen *there* in that larger world I believe surrounds this one. World there, somewhere large beyond imagining—*what is it—was it—where does it go—what next.* A world there. Far, far beyond vast. World impossible to grasp. Impossible as grasping smallness, quickness of being here.

Things that happen here (and there) affect me more or less as they affect anybody, but feel real for me only occasionally, only temporarily these days, when I, or someone like me, a brother, a sister, or like S, or like R, my fellow sufferers, make up a story. Work hard at it. So I feel them there, working. Working word by word.

She was my student, but long ago and in another country. She would arrive during office hours I was obligated by the university to post, three hours a week for each three-credit course I was being underpaid to offer, hours when students could expect teachers to be available and responsive outside the classroom, office hours I routinely skipped or filled with scheduled appointments to avoid wasting time sitting alone in an empty office, or avoid the necessity of conversation unless a student and I had a specific text-in-progress to discuss. She'd be standing in the hall, quiet, patient, waiting to be invited in if my door opened and another student, business completed, filed out.

Maybe hunger for self-expression, for self-empowerment entices students to fiction-writing workshops. But a fiction's first casualty always *self*. Words on the page dismantle self. Writer and reader are suspended temporarily or possibly forever after beyond issues such as self-expression, self-empowerment, or self-improvement. Remain above and below judgment while fiction renders a space that resembles or recalls or replaces or forgets, almost, the unforgiving, elusive, intractable kinds of places that words on a page cannot create. A fiction unfolds and attempts to make itself matter. Pretends something of consequence on its way and will reveal itself. Whether reader or writer exists or not. Whether anybody cares or not. Believes or not.

No, not rich . . . I am a poor man with money, which is not the same thing—words spoken by a character in *Love in the Time of Cholera*, a novel by Marquez I read on another beach. The rich always rich, the character understands. Rich beyond enriching themselves further with anything they might buy or sell. Though the rich continue to spend flamboyantly, flagrantly, greedily, everywhere on anything worthless or not.

Words of stories imitate time. Like a poor man's play money imitates riches of the rich. As if. As if words are able to learn time's language. Translate it. Teach it.

Took years before she could write a narrative about her mother. Or should I say took years before my former student could write about herself writing about her mother's murder. My student younger by decades than I was, student who waited patiently in the hall outside my office. She's famous now, on record in a national magazine quoting advice I once offered her. Different advice than offered her by my colleagues in the university's writing workshop, all of them, every single one of them, as white as I was colored in those days, and not by accident. My colleagues unanimous about the direction my student's writing should take. Same direction as theirs, of course, and they advised her strongly, publicly to follow in their footsteps, in the footsteps of writing they admired, championed, and strove to imitate, hoped to reproduce or exemplify. Advice in all fairness I must admit was well-intentioned, advice that very well may have helped her win the honors she's achieved, but advice that I also considered too colorless, just as they probably would have alleged my counsel too colorful. Their advice as white as they are, I could have grinned at my student, my tongue slightly in cheek.

If I write this fiction about the young woman who was once my student, do I owe readers, tempted to read it, an explanation of why I chose not to tell a tale about made-up nobodies on a beach, but poached instead on the celebrity of my former student, the actual famous person she has become.

Though facts cannot answer my question and certainly facts don't speak for themselves, here are a few facts, anyway. My former student born colored, April 26, 1966, Gulfport, Mississippi—UMass grad writing program 1995—Pulitzer Prize 2007—poet laureate 2012, 2013—her mom, a colored American—dad, a white Canadian—the couple had to travel to Ohio to marry (1965) because in Mississippi, where they resided, mixed marriage a crime—when their daughter, my student-to-be, was six years old, her parents divorced—mom married again—murdered (1985) by second husband, colored, whom she had recently divorced—my student marries eventually—she and her husband are university professors—fire (2017) destroys their just-purchased vintage home during family party—they rebuild—move back three years later, living there now, I presume—must presume because years since we've spoken last—but please, I'm asking, please just bear witness, please, my dear once-upon-a-time student, and maybe help me list more than facts, help me, please, explain why the two of us never bonded more deeply, never became more than a little bit friendly, though, obviously, both of us heirs, then and now, of so many, many shared, overwhelming truths, beauties, atrocities, contradictions.

Each of us might have been the special friend the other yearned for/needed. Special friend in spite of age disparity, gender difference, her choice of poetry, mine of prose. In spite of ugly gossip that would have attended any hints of intimacy between a married (to white woman) colored prof and his colored (or half-colored) student. In spite of the inevitable rumors and told-you-so's, white-hot heat of colored blood, color's need and hunger for color. In spite of every fairy tale and innuendo and tidbit of envy and wishful thinking our hosts could invent about our lives. Those stories, long and short, visible daily, predictably in their eyes when we saw our hosts seeing us. Glances and gazes and stares that enforced an unconditionally incriminating history upon all of us.

So why did we allow ourselves to be categorized, victimized. Why did we never explore together, privately, the secrets we held in common. Air them. Insist upon them. Instead, each of us separately taking on a phony life with a tenacious life of its own that proliferates, dogs us to this very day. Despite our intelligent caution, our power to avoid traps, to choose with circumspection which doors to enter or close, despite our power to distract or ignore or weather or shame or snip off and stomp their wagging tongues.

Neither of us chose to reveal much suffering to the other, did we. If we had shared more, it may have made us closer. And wouldn't being closer have made some things easier. Though in some people's eyes (our own eyes, too?) we were already closer than Siamese twins joined at the hip. But neither of us struggled enough to absolutely refuse and repudiate facile identities thrust upon us by other people, never got around to discussing the hard, cold facts of life our divided lives shared—color, rage, murder of and by family members, our sons, brothers in prison, our fury over tabloid versions of our lives concocted by the press.

During the couple years when you were enrolled in the creative writing program in which I taught, we probably feared and avoided and looked forward to the other's absence in public gatherings at least as much as we welcomed the other's presence. And thus for what we believed damned good reasons, we decided not to break the deepest silences within us, not to disturb silence around us, the silence of others that was intolerably noisy, an unspoken conspiracy generating in them the vigilance and profound ambivalence about color that suffocates, protects, molds them and us. Both of us, you and I, accepting silence as gift, as weight.

What a high price we paid to be accepted or avoided or forgotten or celebrated. Back then—school days, school days, good ole golden rule days—we mostly managed to ignore the price, since lots of other less rotten, less urgent though intriguing, educational stuff, it seemed, to talk about. Less invasive, less troubling, less intimidating and deadly workshop stuff available to converse about so why risk trouble, pain, the unnamable grief of fessing up inner frustrations and festering wounds to one who is hurting already. As you yourself hurt. One too vulnerable, too much like you, too much you.

I worry that perhaps in this new fiction I am contemplating and maybe beginning to write, I will try again to make fiction a substitute, an alternative life competing with, liberating me from a demanding life demanding to be lived. Worry I'm repeating the same mistake, repeating the strategy we deployed for those couple years we had offices on the same floor, my office mine, yours shared by five or six grad students. I worry that fiction—mine, anybody's—too self-consuming. Fiction can't create lives or save lives. Does not change or sort out memories and intimacies of our shared histories, longings, our captivity, the machinations of our ancient enemies. I worry that I will use in my possible story only selected pieces of you to invent a fictional woman eating her lunch on the beach while another fiction (me?) stares out to sea. Me staring at him sneaking stares at her. But I promise in whatever I write not to risk again our lives on a slaveroad. Nor to subject you or myself to complicity again in schemes that perpetuate our dependence upon smothering, protective daydreams of others, others willing to enslave and drown human beings, others who designate their color as *white* and the color of everybody else as *color*, a division entitling *white ones* to mastery, to dominion over *colored ones.*

I will do my best this time, in this story, to accomplish more than simply expressing deep regret about how irresistible, tragic, predictable, inevitable it is for most of us to become lost on the slaveroad. How we internalize and perpetuate the negative imagery in which others drape us, disguise us from one another, even from our own selves, employing us as accomplices in show-trials and executions, beauty contests. Rather than simply telling that sad story all over again, please . . . I will try . . . try what . . . help me, please. My oh my . . . oh shit, shit, girl . . . my oh my, girl, it's been so long, too long since I've seen you or we pressed flesh together—please—a sister and brother.

What power or peace or grace might we have conjured if no sillinesses of fabled romance or doomed romance manqué or happy-ever-after tempted us. Didn't we both know better. Those soap operas never desired, never meant to be. Both of us on our separate paths just wanted to survive the workshop ordeal basically intact, basically more competent in the arts of narrative, but please, perhaps just bear witness with me, my sister and self, to the inscrutability of time, of stories, quickness of time passing—stories passing, lives consumed on this slaveroad, and thank you dearly for your poems and memoirs, and also for listening with attentiveness once upon a time, then years later relating to a journalist the tale I once told you of the Oxford don and fiction writer to whom, when I was his Chaucer student, I showed a couple stories and him telling me (advice infuriating me then, but understood differently now), Yes, yes, yes, fine—down and out in Paris and Spain fine, Mr. Wideman, really gritty, intriguing subjects, but get closer to home. Go home, sir, in your writing.

Stories deliver plagiarisms of death and fear and hopes. Lives—unlike stories—have no beginnings, ends, episodes, nor shape. Not patterns like stories tempt us to believe. As if quantities of time exist like quantities of oil or sugar or breath or sunlight or numbers.

As if more time, different time, perhaps even better time available through more words or dancing feet or painting and sculpture or memories or songs. As if time not like a slaveroad, not a sign of the hidden world encompassing this one.

So home again, home again, jiggety-jig. I need to touch and be touched to the quick—that *quick* nothing separating us from the dead—separating a woman eating lunch on a beach from a man I see she sees on a rock staring at her. Point being to cross un-negotiable distance, cross roads that neither of them—imaginary woman, imaginary man—nor any of us ever crosses, nor gets to *the end.*

And though I understand all the above, I feel compelled to continue my story. What happens after the woman spreads her towel on the sand. What happens to S or happens to R, or happens to Lucy, or happens to Ntomanjela, or to Ntombi . . . etc., etc. Or happens to me, etc., etc. . . . Should I entitle every story—*The End*. Leave behind no other words on the page. Only *The End*. Words stark and stranded as last words of Mistah Kurtz, *the horror, the horror*.

. . . black sheep, black sheep,
have you any wool . . .
yessir, yessir . . . whole head full . . .

Start there. With that. Start with *jump about, wheel about, and jump Jim Crow.* We're all family here, I say, and sing *Farther along.* Sing this old house. Sing this old rock of age.

She is my sister, I say. And please, I want you to be pleased to meet her, my sister, Tish, named after Letitia, daughter of a family for whom my father's mother, Tish's grandmother, worked as housekeeper for many many years, many years ago, my sis Letitia we call Tish for short, always used to call her Tish, anyway, till she married a man of the American Moorish faith and now Charity or Tish or Sis, meet her, please, my sister, Letitia Anne Charity El because she is surely probably pleased to meet you, you my sister writer. Much in common. So please exchange smiles, a hug, because she is my sister in this story and not my sister, too. My sister is not gone, thank goodness, but here and also not here like my incarcerated brother, my incarcerated son, like all my brothers long gone and not here but still in this terrible place. Captive. Imprisoned. Enslaved. This outside like inside. And inside like outside. All of us, inside and outside, confined in little test tube habitations, row after row, or meticulously stacked one atop another, crooked high-rises rising to the ceiling, test tubes sealed with wine bottle corks to keep people inside, inside with potions and poisons that keep a person brewing, stewing to prove whatever happens inside or outside supposed to happen. Don't you see. See it. See them. Us. Testing. Brewing.

And now my hands full of popcorn, bottle of cold juice, sandwich in a warm cellophane pouch as through a crowd of mostly colored bodies I bob and weave back from vending machines toward a far corner of a crowded prison visiting room where sit my sister and mom, the three of us today visiting from outside, visiting my brother inside and he sits there too, in the same corner, beside both his ladies, our ladies, him smiling, very nearly happy because he sits between them, on one of many identical seats in side-by-side racks of four seats each, racks divided and supported and secured to concrete floor of the visiting room by bent black steel rods, white plastic perforated seats molded to approximate and conform no less scientifically than test tube houses conform to general contours of a human form.

Closer to them I see, no, no, don't see, can't be seeing what I see, a tiny puddle in the shade under Mom's seat. Ima big boy, old man now, but despite knowing better than to doubt any terror, any atrocity I encounter in this place I know beyond terrible, I attempt to convince myself, no, I do not see pee behind, below Mom's white seat. Not much anyway. Barely a drop or maybe three. Bowl of perforated seat hardly damp. More like a gleam haloing her trim but heavy bottom where it rests heavily, too heavy for man or god or daughter or son to lift and lead to the promised land of the restroom once the first hour of visiting has expired, too long, too long, too heavy, and you would notice pee, wouldn't you, only if you were staring at a beautiful, fragile, proud old person brave enough to be visiting somebody in this god-awful place where you find yourself, you staring around trying to make sense of why you, they, anybody would show up, let alone linger three seconds here inside this so-called visiting room where a fragile, beautiful, proud old lady sits across from you or next to you or who is you or is your mom and winds up leaking through the safety garment snug around your crotch you hate taping yourself into, your adult Pamper to get you through however long they keep you waiting in line before a visit begins, how long they take—after you are sitting imprisoned in your seat inside the visiting room—to find your son in the prison yard, where you know he was waiting 'cause he's told you, Mom, how it is in here, how they ignore or flat-out deny or tease or on purpose lose you or busy you in make-work with malicious intent and how he's probably been very visible to the guards, waiting, hanging around, just about jumping up and down like a silly kid, making a fool and nuisance of himself since dawn, risking a write-up that might cancel visiting privileges in order he hopes to be sure, sure they can *find* him the moment his mom arrives.

A veteran. You know the drill. The perils. Guys in here or visitors visiting who totally lose it. Just can't take it, can't take the separation and waiting and pain a minute longer and blow up on the brink of a visit. Spoil a visit, forfeit a visit, swear never again, never again.

But here we are, sisters and brothers, no choice. Gathered here again, lunchtime, snack time, because we have not found, nor invented, nor negotiated, nor forced with fire and blood a better way, so here we are again, desperately holding on to the little bit they give us, as if there is no other way but this way, doing as we always have for far, far too long, for years, lifetimes, centuries, and us still doing what they order us to do, where they order us to do it, do it their way, their godfuckingdamn way. Us playing with or swallowing or choking on being what we think they wish us to be, as if no other ways exist, Mom. I am so goddamn sorry, Mom, Sis, Bro, Daughter, Son. So hungry. Bet you are, she say, he say, they say, too.

No it doesn't stink of piss as we sit and chat and giggle and weep and lean over the iron-hard, white edges of our adjacent seats arranged as if side by side the only way in the universe, and no exception here, in this blessed country in which we live, that seats are supposed to be arranged and test tube houses arranged, corked up, crowded in rows or stacked high as the sky, no exceptions to such arrangements, but no, no, no stink in my nostrils, thank goodness, and thank her garment perhaps and thank sweet forever scent of a brave fragile proud old woman's innards, no, the something I dare not mention, but do in fact smell—tears—smell tears dripping from eyes of the sea, salty tears the sea can't help shedding as it rubs over and over against this sandy, rock-studded beach where I sit and imagine a story . . .

We are not only strong, unique individuals, I could have, should have taken my student's hand and said, but a people with our collective understanding of a history we have suffered and endured, stories that belong to us, we have earned them, learned from them, keep them alive in our minds and bodies, and if we share them with each other, with the world, no one can unsay them, take them away from a person, from a people, though murdered one by one or all exterminated.

I remember my brother rising almost immediately after guard at guard's kiosk called out his name and number, my bro up and hovering a moment like a big hovering bird over each of his ladies, gentle strokes and whisperings for each one, and by then me on my feet, too, and we hugged, patted each other's backs before he strode to the kiosk and joined other guys there watching, remembering, staring for as long as they are permitted at visitors like my sister standing now in front of Mom's seat, taking both of our mom's hands in both of hers, *time to go now, Mom,* and no doubt in my mind my lil sis, if she needed to, could lift our mother bodily from that white plastic bucket of seat and carry her out like a baby in her arms, head draped on her shoulder, but she didn't need to because slow, slowly Mom rose and slowly, slowly she straightened, a slow step, then more steps slow, slow, but never wavered, her hand in Tish's hand who went first in front of Mom and me, me close, very, very close behind my ladies, to the doors where you enter and exit the visiting room, doors with machines guarding them that peep under your clothes.

And the story ending there, *The End*, maybe, passing through time, through those visiting room walls and doors maybe, instead of on the beach, man on a rock staring, woman on the sand eating lunch, woman who might be once upon a time my student, best of friends, sister, *The End*, but not ending there on the sand nor here with these other words, in this other place, not *The End*, a different title, different words, more words, a different place because it's a different story, but not exactly, not a story yet and also all stories, all in one, and no story, nothing, I write nothing, only imagine how it might be if I did, guessing again where it starts and ends.

REBEKAH

Ground covered with snow. Rebekah wonders how many pieces of snow it takes to cover the ground.

Flakes their word for pieces of snow falling. Too many to count when sky full of them falling.

Pieces of snow cover the ground and Rebekah wonders if she is looking at *flakes* covering the ground and how to count them if they are flakes and what to call them if they are not flakes covering the ground and how many and why isn't each one seeable as she sees each one when it is falling.

To see snow you must cross the sea. Why, she thinks, and wonders why. Snow far away once. Many seas, many ships far. Too many, too far to count. No one asks the girl she was, the girl whose name others do not say, name they do not ask, no one asks her if she wants to see snow. No one asks her then or now.

When she was little, my daughter said to me her teacher said to the class, *Snow furriers tonight, boys and girls*, and I still see *furriers.*

Snow furriers covering the ground.

They call it snow here, Rebekah says, and pieces of snow falling in the sky are flakes, they say.

She is not anything she can count nor anything anyone else remembers the name of. No one tells her why a ship with her inside its dark belly, why a girl who dies or is sold, sold and dies, sold and lives and dies again and again, must cross seas to see snow covering the ground.

PENN STATION

Information board says train on time. No arrival gate posted yet. I'm running early. Not my usual habit. Perhaps I should admit to myself I'm a bit scared. Perhaps admitting will help. More than a little fear I'm feeling. Feeling dread. Deep down dread. Forty-four years since I have stood next to my brother anywhere outside prison walls, and if the train is truly on time and he is on it and gets off and comes up the underground stairwell and through the steel entrance/exit portal guarding Gate 7/8 West, he will be here, beside me in Penn Station.

My brother said to me once: Worst fear, Bro. My very worst fear is dying in prison. I know dead is dead. When time's up, it's up. But you can't even die right when they got you locked up. A man don't just die in prison. He disappears. He aint nothing. Nowhere. Gone like he never been alive.

I'm remembering my brother's words and wondering if he's relieved now from his worst fear. He's out. On probation. Back. I stare at Gate 7/8 West. Believing, not believing my brother on his way, that he will be among the passengers mounting stairs or riding up an escalator, people scattering, clambering into Penn Station.

Longer I stare, the less I'm sure he will appear, and dread deepens. If I look away from the gate, will it vanish. Will I vanish if I continue to stare. How will I distinguish my brother from the dead. Dead passengers on the slaveroad. Dead people because I don't know them and they don't know me, and couldn't care less, unless we get in each other's way. And if any one of us possessed the power to drift even an instant inside another person, would we really want to. Why risk it. Each one stitched tight into his or her dead uniform like the woman behind a glass wall in an Amtrak smock who informed me that train 42, the Pennsylvanian, en route from Pittsburgh, PA, scheduled for Gate 7/8 West, but check the Information Board closer to arrival time, sir, to make sure, she said, after her eyes rose on a slow escalator to finally meet mine. Shape of eyes, shape and color of her face concealed by umbrella of a bushy 'fro until a single uptilt of her head and a few words suggested that she might be paying attention to a person in front of her and not to a screen, not totally absorbed or dreaming or asleep as she gazed at the console that monitors streaming crowds in subterranean tunnels, the dead scheduled daily to rise and file through Gate 7/8 West's metal arch.

Anxiety mounts as I wait. Later, when I tell people the story of meeting my brother in Penn Station, I try to make it funny, but nothing really funny about two brothers separated from each other forty-four years by prison, and then stranded in a train station for approximately an hour and forty-four minutes, each looking for the other and not finding him. Neither able to pick out the other from the crowd, though probably, when the Pennsylvanian arrived just about precisely on time, the brothers were only approximately forty-four yards apart. Both frozen in place, surrounded by scurrying people, neither one daring to budge and risk missing the other. Then both poor souls wandering, searching the station. Where oh where could the missing brother be.

Maybe the brothers' situation funny, after all, when a public service announcement I always claim that I had requested in my version of the Penn Station story gets claimed instead by my daughter as her idea, and she takes credit for the call that united me finally with my brother and blames me for being a knucklehead every chance she gets in family gatherings when she's around and the story comes up of me in Penn Station unable to find my newly released-from-prison brother and she grins and interrupts me and reminds everybody how old-fashioned, grumpy, and dumb I am about cell phones and internet and why didn't I think to take my cell phone to Penn Station and my poor lost brother wandering around the station upset until he calls her cell phone on his cell phone to ask for help locating me, but of course she didn't have a clue where I might be nor why in hell I had not been at the gate when after forty-four years my brother's train from Pittsburgh arrived, so she, not me, she amends my story, she, my daughter the hero, she reminds everybody, says she called Amtrak and requested the public address announcement that finally brings my brother and me to the Amtrak information booth in Penn Station, where believe it or not, we almost missed each other again in a very small waiting area adjacent to the booth. But then our eyes meet, and we holler, sigh, and hug, and decide to laugh, not cry about a lost, anxious hour and forty-four minutes.

Same way my brother and I used to sometimes decide in prison visiting rooms or during prison phone calls limited to ten minutes to laugh off all the lost time, all the approximately ten . . . twenty . . . thirty . . . forty-some fucking lost years and counting. Aint nothing but a party, like Aunt May used to say when we danced her in her wheelchair. My sweet boys, your sweet mama's sweet babies, life nothing but a party, Aunt May said.

Except somewhere in the middle of the party comes a moment when it's not enough party, not enough fun and dancing and laughing, and in that sudden, quiet quietness, you are alone. Empty. And though not quite ready to jump ship, not quite ready yet for the party to end, no doubt a plunge into dark, cold water strikes you as an appealing, even merciful idea. Maybe icy ocean water would wash away despair, you think. Ocean a color you can't name. Brownish green swirling to darker brown to black with moon-bright patches scudding, churning. Ocean water so goddamn cold that probably cold, cold shock the last and only thing you'd know. Final thing endured for just a few seconds before you are beyond hurt.

Coldness of water that churns its cold way thousands of miles to reach New York City, where ocean laps quietly at stones anchoring a newly constructed scenic walkway along the edge of Domino Park, a place where I often wind up, peering down at salt water forty-four or so feet below the walkway railing, and some days, leaning on the metal rail, I wonder again just how cold the water could be, how long anyone could survive the cold first shock. Wondering if I would go with dignity like Africans I saw in a movie on TV who leapt into the sea first chance from a slave ship. Heads bobbing a second or two in the water, then both arms shoot straight up to the sky while they sink, no regrets, drowning rather than letting strangers steal them from home.

I kick, sprawl, bat water, float, go under, swallow, spit, choke. Water couldn't stay impossibly cold very long, I think. Maybe if you leap, water more like a fist in the face and knocks you out. If anybody watching, it could be kind of funny, I think. I imagine a somebody almost me at the railing in Domino Park who watches my silly, short struggle in the water getting me no place but gone.

Ten years older than my youngest brother when they locked him up. How much older or younger now. Not simply a matter of counting years. I am eighty-one years old and how much older or younger am I now than my dead uncle Ernie, eighty-one when he passed two years ago.

Prison strips away time. Leaves your body bare, bones shivering. No end or beginning to prison time, my brother schooled me. Time shrivels to routine, repetition. Time turned around. The longer your sentence, the less time matters. Prisoners own no time. Only counterfeit time like counterfeit money.

They got it down to a science, man. They real good at making our lives miserable, Bro. Clock time don't stop inside the joint, my brother said, but it's changed, squeezed down till ain't no quality of life in it. Nothing, Bro, even when guys released, time is fucked-up. Isn't real time. Halfway time in a halfway house so feels like you still in jail. Time don't just start up again. Neither can you. You ain't never gone catch up. Never get your time back. Your people back.

So I fret. About my brother's whereabouts. Mine. Second-guessing the book publishing busyness in France that I had treated as urgent and allowed to detain me so I missed my brother's homecoming in Pittsburgh. No peace today for the entire hour and forty-four minutes while I wait, then search for my brother in Penn Station. Worrying about what could have occurred—accident, illness, argument, fight, mean cops, or him just plain lost or maybe he's changed his mind about a visit. Only three weeks since he was released on probation after forty-four years in prison, released into a new, high-tech, gadget-addicted world. Gadgets and world scarcely comprehensible to me. What would they look like to him. Though he was granted special dispensation by Pennsylvania's Department of Corrections for a two-day trip to New York City, why would I expect no glitches, no anxiety. Why wouldn't I anticipate something unimaginably terrible in Penn Station's slaveroad traffic of living and dead.

I search the station for faces of family. Mother. Father. Grandfathers. Grandmothers. Kids. See my great-grandfather posed in his voluminous preacher's robe in a faded sepia photo from Promised Land, South Carolina. See two of my three brothers, both dead now, their faces hovering in shrouded middle distance, then each one flashes crisper, brighter than life, snapshots on an iPhone shoved too near my eyes. As if I don't remember, as if it's necessary to remind me. As if I don't know already my brothers are here and gone. Gone. Gone. See my little sister, who, thank goodness, is still very much alive, despite being the only girl, and being born in the middle, squeezed between two older, two younger brothers. I see her grin. Hear her special way of calling her football star brother *devilish*. Brother with his soft, green-gray eyes, Superman biceps. Brother two years younger than her, eight years younger than me when he held on to my elbow, shuffling his Parkinsonian shuffle down a long corridor inside a nursing home. I see the face of the brother four years younger than me, two years older than Sis, him in a casket in Atlanta, quiet, dignified, shy, handsome as he has always been.

My youngest brother a survivor like Sis and me, but where is he, why is he wandering somewhere unseen in Penn Station. A stray hidden in the crowd. Invisible unless the crowd disperses. Unless it turns on him, turns him out. I'm probably as ghostly to him as he is to me. Both of us maybe a bit afraid of finding the other. Afraid of looking past or seeing through the other's flesh and bones. Same kind of superstitious fear that keeps me from saying my siblings' names aloud or even saying their names to myself in Penn Station. Or writing their names here on this page, as if names are simply words.

Among passersby in the station, my father, all skin and bones. Lifetime of menial jobs consumed his body, embittered his sharp mind, and he's nodding off, head slumped against the elevated back-rest of a hospital bed. Slides down deeper, deeper into waterproof sheets beneath a grayish, papery blanket. Father who loved me but always kept careful, cool distance between the two of us. Distance I'd written and spoken about often. But my father his father also, my lil bro reminded me in a TV interview I watched recently—Daddy only twenty-one, twenty-two years old and boom. He got you, a son to deal with. My big brother. Then I come along, ten years and four kids later, my brother said to the woman interviewing him. Daddy thirty-one, thirty-two years old by then, a grown man then. Lotta difference between how Daddy treated me and how he treated my oldest brother. Best not exactly take everything my big bro says about our father as gospel truth, Miss.

Seeing my father drugged, more or less confined to a bed, I wondered if his sharp mind finally (mercifully) had begun to forget that he had never been granted an opportunity to flourish, never held a job commensurate with his considerable talents and ambitions. Or was his mind still aware, still yearning, still determined, but he was just so so tired, needed to rest, to shut his eyes until an awful world succumbed, a better world glided in to take its place. Isn't that the strong man I heard in his voice. Nothing forgotten or forgiven, even during those last times towards the end when he could barely stand up without help. Man undefeated still. Not the man whispering once from the bed as I was leaving the room, to please take him with me. Please, he said, a *please* too close to begging, and his words, that last *please*, almost broke my will, but I was my father's son and I could let go. Not answer him. Not explain. Not say sorry. I could turn my back on him and leave him behind. My father's son, walking away, not looking back. Not letting my father, not letting my dead brothers, my live son in prison drag me down. Heartbreak a deadweight I bury within myself, shape-shifting my way through guarded doors of the ward that locked my father down.

Couple years ago on a visit home to Pittsburgh I ran into a guy, a long-time-no-see, large, heavy man (soon to die of a heart attack) I used to hoop with back in the day. He'd been a warrior on the court. Several inches taller than my six feet, one-and-three-quarter inches, guy about my age, my color, except several shades darker. In a Kmart parking lot we shared our anger and frustration about the story going round of two cops who, for no reason anybody could justify, had recently shot and crippled a young colored man from our neighborhood. I shook my head, asked my old hoop buddy why these awful things keep happening. Wondered aloud what anybody could do to stop it. His response was to nod, shrug his broad shoulders, raise both big hands chest high, extending them to either side of his body, fingers spread as if to display clean, empty palms. A gesture of helplessness or vast acceptance or maybe surrender or defeat. Shit happens, he said. Not just to us, my man. Shit just happens. Yes, I replied. Shit happens.

Like my encounter with a young man who emailed me in the spring of 2014 and asked in a very humble, decorous, and respectful manner if I might find a minute to meet with him during a visit he would soon be making to NYC. He had recently been selected a Rhodes Scholar and in the fall would be off to England to study literature at Christ Church college, Oxford University. He was reaching out to me, he said, because he had read that in 1963, two of us, Joseph Stanley Sanders and yours truly, were the first Rhodes Scholars of African American descent that the American Rhodes committee had elected to send to Oxford since 1907 when Alain LeRoy Locke was the very first and had remained the only candidate of color deemed worthy of honoring with a scholarship in the ensuing five decades. The young man was quite impressed by what he termed my "historic achievement" and further inspired by the fact I was a writer whose fiction and essays he admired, plus a university professor of English literature, accomplishments, he said that he desired very much to be able, in his own humble way, to emulate.

I emailed back—promptly, positively, probably as curious about him as he seemed about me. Sure!—look forward to meeting you, Field—both our schedules tight and both busy in various parts of NYC while you will be here—maybe Penn Station—accessible easily by subway from most sections of the city—is convenient neutral ground where we can hook up and hang out a bit.

My internet skills primitive and I'm still as wary as I am appreciative of the wonders of electronic tyrannies monitoring and modeling what folks continue to believe are private, intimate exchanges. But my dear daughter, heart of my heart, smart and funny as she can be, not always correct, not always accurate when she gets on my case for being hopelessly behind the times. People change. Even old, grumpy, suspicious fathers. I've more or less happily converted from old-school pen-and-ink first drafts and dependency upon a typist to render them into legibility (for thirty years my first wife, my daughter's mom, the typist), and now I peck out stories, conception to final version, on my iPad.

Subsequent to the young man's flattering, though also daunting, request to meet me, my initial uneasiness, my misgivings regarding the undeservedly high opinion he held of me, my anticipation of the no doubt inevitable crash of the precarious, shaky pedestal upon which he insisted on mounting me, I've discovered he isn't seeking me as a hero to worship. After bumping into him at a couple conferences, a few work-in-progress manuscripts exchanged, emails and phone talks over the years, my esteem for him has heightened and his opinions about me, if only slightly more tempered, are less intimidating. We've become—if not exactly ole buddies and pals—bonded by mutual affection, mutual concern, each of us nurturing an abiding wish that the other—usually far distant one—is well. Keeping up, recommending books, articles.

But Field Brown doesn't appear in this story to offer me an opportunity to repeat to readers his high opinion of me, nor to demonstrate my generous support of upcoming generations of writers of color. Nor am I going to say much more about him as this story progresses. The simple fact is his name the main reason I chose to meet him, and indeed, Penn Station, which *is* one subject of this piece, turns out to be the place where we met. His name, Field, was enough to intrigue me, if truth be told, the sort of off-key, weird shit that grabs my attention, so just learning a guy's name Field was enough to tempt me to rendezvous with him. Field Brown . . . who would stick a name like that on a newborn, especially on a brown kid destined to be raised in darkest Mississippi, one who by chance winds up like me loving books and aspiring to be a writer, and what kind of backcountry Mississippi-mud name a child after a *field*, a *brown* field, and why not a green one so at least maybe the child could pretend to be a rich, Jewish Greenfield and not just any ole impoverished Mississippi Negro of a trifling brown field hue.

Eventually, I learned that Field, the name preferred by the young man who had emailed me, short for Mayfield, his grandfather's name, a man of whom Field inordinately proud, and much more in awe, quite rightly, than in awe of me. His granddad the young man's hero long before Field enamored with me. Donald Mayfield Brown, Field's granddaddy, a farmer, a fabled, successful defender of his community's dignity, prosperity, property, and civil rights back in the days Mississippi colored weren't reckoned to own dignity, prosperity, property, nor civil rights nor the slightest right to insist they should own such, nor protest an inch if they didn't, unless willing to forfeit life altogether and suffer the pain of sudden, ugly death by lynching or crucifixion on a burning cross.

Recently, I asked Field if Sterling Brown a member of his Brown clan, a question I can't imagine why I didn't ask sooner. No, the answer, not family, but renowned Southern-born critic and writer, SB had been read and appreciated by Field Brown. SB a literary presence almost as inspiring for Field as the towering figure of Mississippi's own Richard Wright. Wright world famous, though not sufficiently famous in the USA, Field would argue, like he'd argue as forcefully as I would that Alain Locke, Brown, Sanders, and Wideman aren't proof of a fair competition, but represent just a tiny, tiny bit of playing catch-up. Rhodes folks wearing a nice cop mask for a minute instead of nasty cop mask. As if a smiling face, a few kind gestures cancel history, stop the slaveroad's continuing exercise of vastly unequal power and brute force. Whether the business is evaluating literary reputations or Rhodes Scholars, why wouldn't it remain a one-sided affair if a single, self-appointed, self-interested voice dominates. Same old voice always. Change, catching up not possible as long as we think we're dealing with scores, and not with the presence of incalculable debts that can never be repaid, never reckoned, let alone expressed in numbers. Who could say, who would understand when/if the score ever even. Who's keeping score. Who wins. Who loses. Who says so. Who has been granted the privilege to keep track or lose track. By whom. Of whom.

But Field not inserted here to quibble about scores or sores. This is mostly a Penn Station story, isn't it. Penn Station, where I had suggested we meet, Donald Mayfield Brown and I, to get acquainted. Bon voyage to him and a bit of homage for me. Maybe good luck, a pleasant, off-beat moment for us both to enjoy as the mad beat of these mad contemporary days heats up.

If 11:00 a.m.'s good for you, it's fine for me. Then eleven it is, okay. Good. Good. And so neither of us gets arrested for being a suspicious character lurking on a street corner, my suggestion is, Brown, let's meet underground in the donut shop I used to frequent back when at least twice a week I used Penn Station.

Field Brown. Fair enough, fun enough. Good enough reason to meet inside Penn Station, in the donut shop just beyond the big information board.

During the years I was a regular commuting between NYC and Providence, Rhode Island, I often imagined Penn Station as a vast live creature carving itself deeper and deeper, burrowing into the earth, digging a womb or grave for enclosing itself and endless trains circling within it, for endless passengers lined up to board trains or sleeping inside trains, and of course, think about it, that's what it is and isn't, right. The station, after all, just an enormous hole excavated, laid out, and signposted to be fairly simple to negotiate, so it seems it's actually not a maze or mirage intent on deceiving people.

And once you're down inside the bowels of it, as I am, as I think about Penn Station now, treacherous as it is, maybe still a better idea to meet a person there inside the station, better than the two of us standing around outside Penn Station, waiting and looking for each other, subject to getting shot or busted by cops for loitering on a respectable uptown street corner in an upscale commercial district, suspected of being the sort of litter you'll notice plenty of surrounding you once you are underground yourself, Brown, with vagrants, homeless, the insane folks, hardened criminals, orphans, petty crooks, immigrants, panhandlers, the crippled and deformed or just desperate people down on their luck, or people who have had no luck ever in life except bad luck, the stumbling, mumbling crowds of fugitives that cops drive from certain civilized city streets down into the whale's belly, a false haven because periodically NYC's finest cleanse the station, arrest or drive derelicts, tramps, misfits, etc., back up to the streets when citizens or the press and TV complain of filth, stink, disorder taking over public facilities, anyway, Donald Mayfield Brown, my advice is let's meet inside PS, where, after the escalators deliver you, the entranceway expands rapidly until it divides at the big electronic information board you soon see in front of you displaying train times, etc.

And here's precisely how you find the donut place, Brown. Just keep walking towards the big information board, walking along what used to seem to me an esplanade, the word *esplanade* sounding, feeling right, though I'd only ever read it, not heard the word spoken nor was I sure exactly of the word's definition so looked it up—*esplanade (1) a long open level stretch of ground for walking along; (2) an open area in front of a fortified place*—and yes, my intuition partially correct, *esplanade* revealed something tangible about how being in the belowground space of Penn Station felt to me, though an esplanade with a roof, and one leading to fortified walls that are invisible, walls if you could see them, that resemble the still standing walls of Elmina or Cape Coast Castle or Fort Christiansborg's walls and ramparts, but you just should keep walking, Brown, straight ahead, towards the big board posting train times and information, can't miss it, right in front of you, almost reaching the ceiling, and there the underground walkway I thought of as an esplanade divides into two broad aisles, and the aisle on the right leads to the donut shop.

Field Brown. Fair enough, fun enough reason, so let's meet at an appointed hour in the donut shop that's to the right after you pass the information board with its overhead display of train times, Brown. You can't miss the board, it's directly in front of you, just keep walking straight ahead after the escalators deposit you into the huge cavern Penn Station turns out to be after you descend from the street-level main entrance on Eighth Ave, between Thirty-Third and Thirty-Fourth Streets. Just go to the right of the info board, and soon you will find a donut shop situated in a row of shops, every kind of crap imaginable for sale in the line of shops over against the terminal's right wall, but just stay to the right and continue walking ahead in the direction of the train tracks and you'll soon reach the donut shop where I often used to hang when commuting twice a week from NYC to Providence, RI, to teach a creative fiction class at Brown University, the donut place whose entrance is just a few yards before a white arrow on the wall and the word *Restrooms* in white, too, both arrow and word painted in white to catch the eye and indicate the availability of public toilets if you turn right at the corner after the shops, but don't turn, because there, just before the long jumble of shops terminates, there where you could make a quick run to the loo if necessary, you'll see a large neon Krispy Kreme sign in the window of one of the last shops. You can't miss it, can't miss them, Krispy Kreme sign and white restroom sign and arrow, and I'll be there in the donut shop that comes a few steps before the signs, and you said you'd know my face from book covers, didn't you, but just to be sure, I'll be wearing a Brown University brown baseball cap. Looking forward. See you soon, Brown.

Not as soon as we both thought. Penn Station jinx, I might call it now. Or slaveroad. Or whatever. You, Brown, sitting in one donut joint, me in another. Missed each other. An accident, or bad luck or fate or maybe I neglected to say Krispy Kreme or said Dunkin' Donuts or you forgot and substituted one for the other or maybe no one can trust their eyes and ears in PS or maybe shops shuffling as shops do and changing names like people do and nobody can find them.

We wasted forty-four minutes or so. Enough time for me to get up from my seat in the Krispy Kreme donut bar and circle the whole bottom floor of the main underground area, once, twice. Shit, I was starting to think, and about to say fuck this, it's not that important, anyway. This Brown kid's on his way. And I was correct. Would learn that you don't need advice from a secondhand, second-story grandpa. Got one Big Pops already bigger than life, back in Mississippi. All a boy needs.

Isn't Penn Station simply a vast public service arena that operates quite well enough for by far the majority of citizens who require its services. No. Scratch the surface, peep beneath the surface, and you don't even need to be seized as I occasionally am by a fit of particularly fevered imagination. Just scratch the surface and what is happening just below the surface becomes clearer. Send me to Oxford. Send Brown to Oxford. Brown passes through Oxford and he stays Brown. As I passed through Oxford and stayed me. Brown stays Brown. I stay brown me. Oxford stays Oxford.

During his first term as a Rhodes Scholar attending Oxford and residing in Christ Church, Donald Mayfield Brown complains to college officials about the racial prejudice he often encounters in his interactions with college workers. The Christ Church administration fires back. Admonishes B for stirring up trouble, particularly among the faithful workers called scouts or porters or custodians who serve and care for undergraduates in the Oxford dormitories. (In my days at New College, Oxford, those scouts aka *pee-ladies*. My *pee-lady* what I called my porter Reggie—though, of course, never to his face—my porter Reg certainly dead by now, the old, arthritic, but rider-still-of-his-bike-nevertheless-miles-to-work-each-day guy who kindly looked out for me and schooled me *re*: quaint customs and intricate rituals for achieving a relatively comfortable undergrad life in miserable, medieval dorms—*pee-ladies*, the traditional, insulting name, inherited and passed on by generations of students, a term perhaps commemorating ancient eras of chamber pots when young masters in training learned they need not dirty their own hands to dispose of their wastes, but could depend upon the available, appropriate, dirty hands of others to do their dirty work, hands of a part-janitor/part–personal servant/part–guardian of the college interests, whose duties included not only *pee-lady* women's work but spying and informing on us if we broke rules such as no female guests overnight or too much drinking or excessive noise or whatever.)

Turns out an Oxford student newspaper chose to feature a story detailing Brown's unhappiness about prejudice he said he was experiencing within Christ Church, and included in the article accounts of other students of color who shared B's discomfort, dissatisfaction, and disappointment, his perception that systemic racism diminished the quality of life at Oxford. The article also criticized the lame reaction of university officials to B's complaints and quoted the response of The Very Reverend Dean of CC: "We are sorry that some members of the University appear to have felt it inappropriate to be asked to show their University cards. At the beginning of any academic year, it is normal practice for our Custodians and Porters to ask to see proof of identity on a regular basis for the first month or so. This is an especially busy time for tourism, and there are still large numbers of visitors walking around. As a newcomer to Christ Church myself, I have been asked to show my ID on entry on several occasions, and I applaud the thorough and professional approach taken by our porters and custodians. Our staff are drawn from a very wide range of ethnic backgrounds. They do a superb job of welcoming students, visitors, tourists and worshippers from all over the world."

Sometime after the student newspaper story appeared, Christ Church issued a public apology. I intend one day soon to check in with Brown and ask him exactly how long it took the college to respond. Ask him if CC officials ever apologized to him personally. Ask him if any significant changes transpired after CC promised to try to do better in the future.

Public apology an ideal solution from Christ Church's point of view. Apology would restore the college's dignity and moral authority. And apology (heartfelt or not) doesn't obligate the college to compensate Brown for injuries sustained when a college dean originally dissed him and dismissed his plea for help. Apology says trust me. Believe me. Says safe to return to business as usual.

Who knows what evil lurks in the hearts of men . . . That's a quote, Brown, from one of my favorite shows I listened to in the kitchen after dinner on my mom's radio when I was a kid. Alone, kitchen light switched off, then my magic shows appeared—*The Shadow, The Lone Ranger, Gang Busters.* Same radio from which my mom's soaps issued daily and gospel music many mornings and often during the day, and on Sundays before and after church, if the family made it to church that Sunday, and we usually did. I still believe only the Shadow knows what evil lurks in the hearts of men. Believe such knowledge beyond the understanding of ordinary human beings like me and you, Brown, though many of our fellow citizens perceive us not as exactly human beings but shadows passing through their lives.

The Christ Church apology is a part of the public record now. So what. I can't pretend to know what the Shadow knows, can't see directly into my own heart and mind, let alone somebody else's heart and mind, Donald Field Brown, so I won't declare CC officials guilty and condemn them without incriminating evidence in hand. But did those good-souled CC folk who issued a public apology worry themselves about the likelihood that an apology's inherent passivity might reinforce, aid, and abet the exclusion Field Brown alleged. Didn't they realize that apologies are not necessarily indicative of soul-searching and self-reflection, but often a means of avoiding them.

Same ole shit. A college, a university, asserting and taking advantage of its privileged position, rather than questioning its ancient, traditional, hallowed role as judge, jury, and executioner of students. Same ole shit. Whether apologizing or drubbing or abusing or educating or excluding you, Brown, the same old institutional prerogatives remain in place. Steady, deadly, unyielding. Relentless as a slaveroad crossing seas.

Same ole shit, *SAMO*. I nod at Jean-Michel Basquiat (aka SAMO), nod at Brown, and Brown nods back, the two of us, three of us standing outside looking inside, or inside looking out, pondering what is and is not inside and outside power's charmed circle of impenetrable, unchanging power. Oh, you motherfucking powerful power, we scribble on stone walls.

Is Penn Station truly jinxed. Truly designed to waylay and disorient. Keep the boy running, to borrow a phrase from Ralph Ellison's *Invisible Man*. Penn Station may do precisely that. Do it to me anyway. To me and perhaps countless others doomed along with me in my pumped-up imagination when I'm seized by notions of conspiracy, of slaveroad. Clearly, institutions allegedly supposed to organize and stabilize and serve society—institutions like Penn Station, Christ Church, the Rhodes Trust—also serve to keep a few of the very powerful, very rich (riches and power indistinguishable in a certain tiny class) in place, keep the multitudes of the rest of us confused, busy, busy while we try to do the bidding (follow directions) of the powerful.

But we do get a last laugh about Penn Station. You, Field Brown, pop up from whatever donut shop you were sitting in when finally you see me pass by. You holler. Rush up on me from behind, big smile on your face when I turn and see you. Professor Wideman, Professor Wideman, sir. Hey, sir. How are you, sir. Thank you so much for coming, Professor Wideman. Afraid I'd missed you. I'm Field Brown. So happy to see you, sir.

Brown, I was thinking, thinking about my days teaching at Brown and thinking about being brown and Brown growing up brown down home in Mississippi and donuts and names and how large, how filthy Penn Station. Thinking how easy, after all, to get lost. And how everybody, especially everybody at the bottom of the heap, gets lost in Penn Station. Last laugh is both of us laughing together at one or the other's joke. Here we are in NYC, this pair of us, both supposed to be scholars, gentlemen, super-endowed, serious, mind-bogglingly bright, brown individuals, and couldn't even figure out how to meet up in Penn Station. No wonder those Rhodes turkeys ration the number of scholarships they give coloreds like us. Maybe they got it right after all, Brown.

In Penn Station, about seven years later, it took me way too long to notice that my youngest brother's slow, obviously painful, gimpy gait was not improving. My plan had been to forgo a taxi and, as a special treat for my fresh-from-prison bro and me, to hop on the F train. An instant, exhilarating immersion for the two of us in the Big Apple, the pair of us united again, inseparable forever, shoulder to shoulder, superheroes ready for anything New York City could cook up in its subterranean bowels. Two fearless adventurers exploring the urban jungle, the moon, whatever. I should have been aware of what a bad idea that was even before a relatively short dash to catch the F train, my brother following me up an escalator, through dense crowds, numerous flights of stairs, near collisions with bodies hurrying to catch subways and trains, me paying no attention to my brother, assuming he was beside or right behind me, until obviously he wasn't, and a long glimpse over my shoulder clarified the fact that I'd missed or worse ignored how much each stride, precarious and halting, taxed my brother. Then shame, colossal anger at myself for not even beginning to understand that, indeed, my brother was back. Exactly him, and nobody else.

In Penn Station, arms wrapped around my brother's body, how easy it had been to forget forty-four years. Forget how those years had changed him, me, and then me, rushing through the station. How unforgivable not to have remembered. Not to have taken appropriate looks, care, caution. Not to have made appropriate adjustments for his sake and mine.

I will make amends, I kept repeating to myself, after I slow down, and my brother catches up beside me, both of us heading directly at the same easy, measured, shared pace for the endless line of taxis outside Penn Station's main entrance. Promised myself to remember the necessity of reconnecting slowly and with extreme care. Repeated to myself how I must learn to watch and listen to a brother who had already forgotten more than I would ever learn about being forgotten. How for forty-four years he had to suffer, no choice, suffer precisely what others determined as possible and not possible for him.

His role for forty-four years to endure, accommodate, survive. To be grateful when the spirit in another person—brother, sister, keeper, stranger—appeared willing to pay some sort of attention to him. To assist him. No matter how wrongheaded, no matter what caused the other to act decently towards my brother, he must smile and show gratitude. Because he needed them. As I need him now, as he requires me now, and requires many other souls, people better and stronger than me, to aid him, help him unbreak himself, put himself back together with severely damaged parts. The necessity for both of us to fabricate new models of ourselves for a new, nearly incomprehensible world.

In the cab on the way from Midtown to my apartment on Grand Street, Lower East Side, after the dumb mix-up and intense delay in Penn Station, my brother asked first thing if I had been to Arizona lately to visit his nephew.

Your nephew, my son, I said. Been way too long since I've seen my son.

You know, Bro, I worry sometimes me being in jail might've messed with him.

He's my son and your nephew, and he and I both say thank goodness for family. That's what we both say. He loves us both, and he has learned like you—probably mostly from you—to be strong. He won't allow prison to destroy him. I'm off to Arizona in two weeks.

Going along to get along, my brother had told me once, the phrase guys in jail used when they were wondering, thinking aloud about how, if and how, they could get through one more excruciating instant. Then another. My brother probably would have limped step by step beside me or behind me in Penn Station for forty-four miles or till he dropped, if I hadn't figured out the obvious and let go my fantasy subway excursion—Cab, fool . . . a goddamn C-A-B, you damn fool . . .

After the cab, after a bumper-to-bumper creep through Midtown then Lower East Side streets, after a big hug for him from my wife, the two of them embracing, not wanting to let go, all smiles, and tears shining like smiles, standing, swaying in the middle of the living room as she hugged him and he hugged back, after my brother had settled down on the couch and kicked back and tried maybe with one deep, deep breath to make up for forty-four years of never enough air in his lungs, after he leaned forward, elbows on knees, leaning that way for more than a couple minutes before he settled back again, not in the middle of the couch, but in the corner he'd chosen, corner shadowed a bit at the end of the couch, shadowed end of the room that had become as quiet as he was quiet while he looked at me and my wife, both of us seated, facing him on wooden chairs pulled out from under the wooden dinner table that divides our apartment's kitchen and eating space from the living room, and then after nobody had spoken a word it seemed for a very long while, my brother said, Bro, you know this the first time since I've been out I feel really free. Really, really free. Here sitting on your couch and no place I got to be tomorrow morning.

JOE WOOD

Nothing unhappens. Asked by an editor to suggest candidates for a new collection of my previously published nonfiction, my initial reaction was *who needs it*—the *who* including in the first place, as usual, myself: Why task myself to stir up memories and revisit thoughts and ideas that I probably would just as soon forget, if I'd not already forgotten. Old words nobody else needs either. Writing largely ignored by the reading public when it originally appeared in print—commissioned essays, bits of memoir, lit crit, social and political commentary, woe-is-me victim statements protesting the outrageous, murderous discrimination still visited daily upon people who supposedly enjoy the equality promised by democracy, guaranteed by America's Constitution and Bill of Rights.

What would be the point of dredging up and displaying pieces of writing that would commemorate and expose my futile attempts to make sense of a world I sought to understand once upon a time, but no, no, did not ever understand, not then, and, more certainly, understand even less now, no, no, not then, not now, so even if I could somehow resurrect my crumbling powers of recollection and struggle through the ruins to revisit whatever I thought I understood once, the results, no doubt, would be embarrassing. So who needs it. What would be the point for me or anybody else to be subjected again to inevitable disappointment. To again read or ignore or dismiss or remain oblivious of irrelevancies whose sole effect has been nil—aside from allowing an author to flaunt vanity and maybe earn a few pennies, a few dollars maybe for the publisher. Nil.

Nil in this nation that continues to conceive and separate its citizens in terms of black or white or mixed, the very same myths of inborn division and inferiority, same mythological colors that rationalized enslavement of millions of Africans, disguised slavery's crimes against humanity for four hundred years.

Nothing unhappens. Hitler doesn't unhappen. No matter how vociferously we may disclaim him or deny or condemn or excoriate or cry never again, never again, or forget or transform or lie about him and ourselves, Adolf Hitler and the genocide he organized doesn't unhappen. Like slavery doesn't unhappen.

Nothing unhappens. Time changes mysteriously. Eternally it seems. Changing beyond any notion of change human minds able to conceive. No starts, stops, beginnings or endings, no numbers, no markers we invent capable of diminishing let alone solving the puzzle of time, of extricating one moment from another, this moment from the last one or from the next one, your moments from mine, my death from yours or any other's death or life.

Just here, there, gone. Always separate. Always conflated, always elusive, always changing too fast to follow or get ahead of or anticipate. Time embodying irreversible paradoxes—simultaneous presence and absence, now and not now, the same and different. Intractable, intangible. Too swift, too fleeting, too immense, too much with us to grasp. Not in new forms, not as old forms revised. A rush, a rip and roar or vast silence or emptiness between next and next. And nothing unhappens.

In this context, undecided about how to proceed, driven more by simple curiosity than enthusiasm for the suggested project, I dutifully read through a list of my former publications an editor had compiled. My reaction to the list: a numbing wave of sadness and disconnection. Except for some reason two unincluded pieces immediately came to mind: the preface to an anthology of Gulf Coast folktales Zora Neale Hurston had collected; an essay I'd contributed to a book about Malcolm X. What exactly I'd endeavored to express in neither of those unlisted essays asserted itself, but both announced quite clearly they were missing. Perhaps I was simply looking for company, seeking some form of substance and reassurance from major figures like Hurston and Malcolm to whom I had carefully listened and from whom I'd learned so much. Perhaps I was hoping their renewed presence, and my remembrances of their giant gifts, might provide a bit of relief from long-distance loneliness, the sense of wasted time and failure as I interrogated myself about what my own writing had achieved.

The internet produced—after I had suffered through numerous of my typically bumbling searches—pictures of the covers of both the Hurston and Malcolm books, and offered reams of numbing information: publication dates, reviews, copies for sale, sample pages, etc. I recalled immediately how much I'd liked the image on the cover of the paperback edition of Hurston's *Every Tongue Got to Confess* and, twenty years later, liked seeing it again. A stylized portrait of Zora Neale standing outdoors, alone, her face profiled, shadowed under a yellow, wide-brimmed country straw hat as she gazes back over her right shoulder, a book pressed to her chest, her figure neat, precise, wearing an open-necked blouse tucked into a long skirt or maybe it's all a single garment, shimmering against an impressionistic background of colors almost repeating the hues, tones, the flow of dress down from her waist to the bottom edge of the picture frame. Browns and golds of skin, of fabric, of landscape blending, transforming each other to suggest the subtle magic of H's rendering of plain folks' everyday speech into luminous words on a printed page.

No memory of the 1991 Malcolm cover when I googled it, and nothing recalled about my essay's content, only the rather unsettling reminiscence that when I had not found the Malcolm piece included in the list of candidates for possible republication, I had not remembered right away the name of the guy who had invited me to contribute to his Malcolm anthology. Able only to recall that he was not a very big guy, soft-spoken, articulate, and a bit shy, and how easily we had become friendly, respectful of one another so that when I heard in 1999 he'd disappeared while bird-watching in the wilderness somewhere near Mt. Rainier, I was shocked, couldn't believe it. He was gone. Stayed gone. So reluctantly, I must have filed the fact he was missing, though I guess I believed I had not closed the file on him. Mourned him in my fashion, lamented his loss, and appreciated gratefully the gifts he had acquired at a very young age and generously bestowed upon a fragile community of writers and readers. Quite ashamed then, thirty years or so later, because it would take me a day or so to say to myself, *Joe Wood.* To put a name on a faded face, the name of a valued person whom I'd assumed I wouldn't ever actually need to name since we'd so quickly, naturally developed the sort of intimacy that seems to transcend names and words.

Joe Wood. Joe Wood, of course. *Joe Wood*, I'd said to myself, surprising myself when his name at last popped into my mind the day before I saw it in an image of his book's cover the internet delivered to my iPad. Joe Wood missing for over twenty years and counting, but an electronic site (more loyal, humane, solicitous than yours truly) announced and preserved his presence, and also featured ads listing prices and places so that interested parties could purchase and own a Joe Wood book about Malcolm.

By recalling Joe's name, I had done him no favor. He was gone, gone. Imagining benefits I might gain from rereading the Malcolm essay Joe had commissioned or rereading my Hurston piece did no favors for the idea of committing myself positively to the project of reviving my previously published nonfiction. Vastly more than dire reservations about that project continue to resonate profoundly. Again and again I ask myself, What would be the point of a new collection. *So what?* My old words wouldn't be salvaged by adding or subtracting essays from the list an editor had compiled. Repeating words doesn't bring them back from the dead, any more than repeating *Joe Wood, Joe Wood* returns him from the snow-packed mountains where he'd gone missing. Weren't my memories of Joe as arbitrary, as selfish and contrived as an internet display. Better probably for me, more respectful to him, to let Joe go, let those once-upon-a-time published essays RIP.

But Joe Wood remains here on my mind. Moved in. Demands attention. Joe, aided and abetted by indescribable forces inside and outside me, stays around. Those forces at work constantly, mysteriously, simultaneously inside and outside of people. Of me. Forces, of course, residing always somewhere else, but wherever else they could be, they also do reside in me. If not in me, who else experiences those forces. If they are not inside and outside of me, where would they be. What would they matter or mean to anyone or to me, if there was not a me. Not *me.* Not mine. Forces where? What forces? Force of whatever passes through me as I pass through.

Joe Wood not an obsession—what's occurring *re*: his name, *re*: him, feels more akin to an energy French surrealists theorized as fundamental to artistic creation and called *hasard objectif*—a pattern of coincidences too intertwined, too revelatory, too unexpectedly connected to be accepted or understood as purely coincidental—an odd sort of conversation around you, within you, in a language you don't speak, a language of inscrutable words, some of which you believe you must have heard before, words maybe you understood once and maybe nearly make sense again, words and phrases and rhythms mysteriously addressing you—and you surprised, close to clairvoyance, close to grasping hidden messages that are suddenly, without warning, being delivered, and meant in an obscure fashion almost certainly for you.

A pattern, a network of more than random convergences emerge as I hear myself saying *Joe Wood.* Couple weeks ago I read an article about Unity, that 1999 conference of Afro-American writers, academics, editors, journalists in Seattle, Washington, the conference Joe Wood attended and from which he never returned. I learned that Senator Bill Bradley, who was campaigning for president of the United States, had, like Joe, traveled from the East Coast to convene with A-A literati, intellectuals, activists, hangers-on, well-wishers, and dedicated foes gathering in Seattle. Obviously, one of Sen B's goals at the Unity event must have been to convince the attendees and their constituencies that he was the presidential candidate most informed, most attuned and sympathetic to urgent issues of race and racism Americans should be compelled to confront at that crucial moment of choosing a national leader. Another article I read that mentioned BB's presence at the Unity event also noted that the senator, when informed JW had gone missing, remembered meeting Joe Wood at the conference and recalled being quite impressed by him.

Just so happens I encountered BB in 1963 as an opposing forward on a college basketball court, then in 1965 as a fellow Rhodes Scholar at Oxford, and now he's a longtime buddy with whom at this very moment I'm sharing thoughts and frustrations about the difficulties of self-representation in the writing occupying each of us: me in my latest fiction/nonfiction narratives; Bill in a dramatic monologue he's performed live onstage, an intimate presentation of his life and career he is composing that will serve also as the basis, he hopes, for a film script and TV documentary. Next time we talk, I'll surely inquire about Joe Wood.

Poking around in news stories and magazine articles that offered accounts of Joe Wood's disappearance, I discovered an insightful, provocative eulogy of JW that I found to be as unforgiving as it was eloquent and challenging. The piece was haunted, terminally suspicious—was Joe murdered by hateful white bigots, self-appointed guardians of Seattle's rigid segregation, of Mt. Rainer National Park's pristine, unspoiled, uncontaminated glories, a party of dedicated, rugged outdoorsmen suddenly transformed into a lynch mob when they chanced upon a colored man violating their sanctuary, or did Joe slip on the ice and plunge into a ravine, but if he did, why didn't rangers and cops and dogs searching for him unearth any clues, find his body or its remnants, and why would smart Joe naively venture unprepared too far into a well-known, precarious, deadly dangerous natural environment, or was Joe, as one female friend alleged, attempting to walk away from a hoard of nobody-else's-business career crises, love crises, failing talent crises, or as some commentators suggested, could Joe simply have been an unlucky victim of Rainier's unpredictably ugly, high-altitude weather.

By coincidence the author of the touching, dissatisfied remembrance turned out to be a person I had communicated with years earlier, Major Jackson, a fine poet, good friend of thirty-four-year-old old Joe Wood when Joe went missing, his age-mate like my son, who was thirty-one years old in 1991, the year JW's book on Malcolm was published, my first son who also writes fine poems, and appeared in an anthology with his colleague and acquaintance Major Jackson, my son three years younger than Joe Wood, son who emailed me re: Joe Wood, "knew of him but didn't interact much," both young men belonging to an informal cadre, along with numerous other women and men, including academics, convicts, politicians, preachers, revolutionaries, street organizers, émigrés, immigrants, jazz musicians, pop singers, rappers, incarcerated folk, etc., etc., a mixed-bag crew of them constituting an up-and-coming, vital salient of A-A culture, many of whom were acquainted through Cave Canem or similar university-based institutions dedicated to fostering associations, fellowships, mentor/mentee relationships at the cutting edge of A-A artistic exploration, a burgeoning, expansive moment announcing perhaps, as many of us in previous generations wished, a second renaissance, an immense flowering of youthful talent dwarfing the Harlem Renaissance that Rhodes Scholar Alaine Locke had described happening around him nearly three-quarters of a century before.

About a month before I had been struck by the fact that my H and M essays were not included among those an editor was considering reprinting, I had written the author of a new book on Frantz Fanon thanking him for his careful, intelligent study of F's life and achievements. Heartfelt congratulations since I had written a Fanon novel. The author had responded by expressing his gratitude and requesting my permission to quote me in the promotional material he was organizing to help sell his book. Emails are passing back and forth between us now to clarify and negotiate how he can make public my words praising his treatment of F without violating my unqualified stance against the commercialized, self-serving, circle-jerk, publishing-house-sponsored endorsements of authors blurbing other authors books. In the midst of these negotiations, in a literary journal, I came across by chance a thoughtful, quite personal reminiscence the Fanon biographer had written about Joe Wood.

I share Joe Wood's fondness for long solitary walks. Wonder which came first, his taste for walking or passion for bird-watching. Probably an irrelevant question. Like asking which one of two lovers determines what happens between them. Point always being reciprocity, being complementariness, being improvisation and spontaneity while lovers are attracted to each other and discover, unpeel, peek at the formidable unknowns they are sharing.

At home in NYC, I power-walk the streets, bridges, stroll in parks along the water, and while here in Brittany, where my wife and I reside for half the year in Le Moustoir, a tiny suburb of Arradon, itself a small town twenty minutes from a bustling commercial center, Vannes, population fifty-three thousand, a seaport from which the notorious slave ship *Diligence* was launched, a city about two and a half hours by train from Paris, here in France, when I walk, I'm able—just minutes after I exit our cottage—to shed Le Moustoir's tidiness, escape what sometimes hits me as the almost sepulchral, cemetery quiet exuded by L M's neat dwellings, manicured lawns, decorative, precisely trimmed hedges and trees, homes not constructed it appears to me for teeming lives, but houses that are monuments to finished lives, homes empty of life as graves, and most days if I choose, and usually I do choose, I can go long stretches and seldom see other human beings as I walk through enormously fertile farmland bounded by low, rolling hills and vast uncultivated fields, through tame woods, or patches of old forest with massive trees that feel primeval, untouched since creation's dawn, darkly frightening almost to somebody like me who grew up in an urban setting like Pittsburgh, or I can choose to trek along rock-strewn or sandy beaches, look out beyond my shoulder at the Gulf of Morbihan, gleaming, spreading towards the horizon to meet open sea.

Yesterday, after not a single soul for forty minutes or so, I noticed ahead of me two figures on the abandoned rural road I was using to reach the highway. My pace faster than theirs and I was gaining ground on them, probably pass them long before the highway intersection and deep woods beyond, but anyway, as I closed the distance between us, approaching them from behind, they stopped, and stood mucking about, on the left-hand edge, from my point of view, of the cracked asphalt surface of the road we were sharing, the two of them occupied, doing something where the old road bordered by a high wall of trees and dense undergrowth.

Couldn't tell much about the pair when they halted, still too far away, but gradually, one of them clearly a man wearing the cliché of a striped Breton jersey tucked into his bulky, below-the-knee-length shorts, cliché of sturdy, tautly muscled Breton calves displayed, slanting inward from invisible knees, so he appears bowlegged like some women back home look in their dresses. Him bowlegged with plenty of room beneath his big shorts for a sleek, strapped-to-thigh sheath holding a bowie knife, and as I approached closer, I could finally discern that the other person definitely a she, no doubt about it, I could tell she was female, as tall as her man partner, her husband friend lover neighbor sibling, whatever they were to one another, a woman bean-pole tall, straight up and down, standing sideways peering at the guy with an apple in his fist, she is a she, as surely as he's a he, though only a painter's hasty stokes, shorthand gibberish of marks, dots, spatters, pale flesh exposed here and there to substantiate her gender, a shorthand like my gaze's shorthand running up and down the long pole length of her body, the tall easel displaying her on a canvas, not more than a foot's width of her, profiled, pictured, an artist's approximation standing there real before my eyes at the edge of the road, slashes of quiet color, ripples, dashes, shorthand for a slim, understated female form.

They are haters. Killers. Murder me and drink my blood. Quickly. Man good with his blade. My throat slit. Belly sliced open. A pro. Gotcha, dude. No need to rub it in. Make you suffer. Over and out. Except both of them pause to exchange a taste of my blood. A wiggly tongue probes, then thrusts through the other's lips. To share. Sample together. Unlike apple he'd been munching and offered her, then tossed away, or black, pebbly-skinned berries she'd tested a few of, biting, swallowing to confirm their ripeness.

When I caught up and passed them, the three of us tried out smiles, abbreviated, easy, hey look at us, aren't we all nice happy folks out here in the Breton countryside engaging in civilized chatter, a patois of creolized English and French, the subjects maybe weather, or no subject at all, just easy patter and shuffle back and forth of nothing words, the little moment we share in which we assure each other, accost each other not much longer in duration than taking a deep, deep breath, which was perhaps all that the three of us side by side, face-to-face, needed to do, putting everything on pause for a few seconds during the rapid glide, slide past each other, a moment lasting approximately no more or less than one, two, three, go and stop and go. A deep breath, some chattering, then them behind me and me on my way away from them, hopefully far, far away from ever running into them again.

There's much more bottom-line, weighty stuff I could cite, stuff not simply accidental like *JW*, the initials Joe Wood and I happen to share. Other significant things, surreal and not, that point onward and upward, ideally, hopefully, beyond the kind of silly joke of *JW*, headed-nowhere stuff. Things more like the infinite, still unfurling human possibilities connecting us all, intimately, globally, those grounded reasons for listening to Joe Wood, talking to him, including the fact that in West Africa the Igbo people argue that as long as a person is spoken about, that individual does not perish. The Igbo also believe as my Igbo colleague at Brown University Chinua Achebe famously contended "all stories are true." Or if not exactly "true," the Igbo language, an Igbo proverb, claims, every person's story has worth.

The extent and meaning of Joe Wood's story, and perhaps the stories I have told and written and continue to write, do not unhappen. And if for no other reason than their existence, perhaps, they deserve to exist. Deserve not to be discarded or forgotten. But being who we are will be discarded and forgotten if we perform submissive rituals, or conform to external mandates, or succumb to pride and vanity and welcome somebody else's flattering/demolishing versions of ourselves, versions that others propose, versions whose purpose is to untell us, censor us, and thus erase and deny our responsibility for ourselves. If we deny our acts, our history, our words, our fears about others and ourselves, we may very well lose precious parts of multiple truths holding, keeping us all alive. Our homes, families, nation, dreams alive on this treacherous slaveroad we all ride.

We risk mortal peril when we choose—and we may, we very well may choose, for various very strong, very wrong reasons (among them constant, unrelievable insecurity or truly believing, accepting the innate inferiority, inadequacy, dependency invented and instilled by slavery, and suffering the persistent anxieties about who and what we are that the slaveroad's unbroken presence stimulates)—choose foolishly to back away, to retract. Shut up. But if we forget, if we stop, if we hide, if we retreat, if we pretend that the stories we tell, stories telling us cannot be silenced, that they are immune and will always speak as once we wished them to speak, and that their truth will abide forever, then Joe Wood is gone gone, irretrievably gone, because we will have surrendered, because we will have forfeited power we once seized. Once expressed. Power—the power once and once again of words continuing to be spoken, written, invented, danced, emblazoned, carved, moaned, missed, misconstrued, sculpted, sung, new words, old words, words in flight, words struggling to name, and naming themselves one more time.

Joe Wood. Hey, man. Here I am, man. Here, Joe Wood. Here. And you are here, too, wherever else you are besides here within and outside of me. Hey, Joe Wood. You are here, man, and here are some essays (tries) I performed once. Tried. I did. Essays. Yes I did. Try. I did. And do. Must. They are me. IOUs, Joe Wood. No expiration dates. Thanks.

CHUNNEL

The less he remembers, the more he must write . . . *bluebirds over . . . white cliffs of Dover . . . wait and see.* Doo-wop. Doo-wop. The alternative is nothing. A life with all those years passing and nothing. Remembering less and less. Nothing, no one there. Year after year. Too many to count. Years beyond counting. Counting less and less. Each one. The sum total. Why bother with numbers as if numbers can keep track. Years empty and more emptiness on the way. The way a mirror is empty unless or until a reflection troubles it, reflections appearing only if one's eyes look and see. Same eyes a sensible person knows are not in the mirror, though if the person looks and sees, yes, yes, eyes stare back as if they belong to a person in the mirror who stares back, a person who is really not a person, but a reflection, not the one to whom the eyes and the looking belong. Then who is looking. Where is that living, breathing person to be found. If ever found. The one who, if seen, is only a reflection. Not visible anywhere, in fact, except in a mirror. Where oh where, indeed.

But his body visible, isn't it. Most parts (arm, finger, knee, nose, etc., etc.) anyway, visible to his eyes. And visible, of course, for other eyes, others might say, might insist. But if the eyes of others are not remembered, if they themselves are spaces blank as a mirror until a reflection is imposed upon it, perhaps those eyes he sees looking don't belong to living, breathing people, just images a person must stare past, stare through when a person looks for herself or himself in a mirror. As when he seeks himself there, free of the eyes of others.

So sing doo-wop. Listen to the song. Ask who sings it. Ask if it matters who is singing. He can hear it, can't he. The song. The singing. It is not nothing. Not nothing like the emptiness in a mirror. Nothing there. No song in a mirror. Silence. Mirror not reflecting a song, not anything, not holding anyone, anything, anywhere. It's empty unless you look and see, then nothing again when you look away.

Not seized. It seizes him. This doo-wop song, this alternative instead of nothing. This alternative of listening to himself listening. Or not exactly listening, because also singing, singing along not quite silently within vaster silence and quiet of a song. Singing, *bluebirds over white cliffs of Dover*, so he's not nothing, so he's something, as if remembered from years and years ago, something saved, recollected, belonging somewhere words may help uncover. Words that are lyrics of a song. Words he writes when he remembers nothing else. Words some doo-wop group's tenor sings falsetto—Dells, Drifters, Diablos, he can't recall which group—a high tenor voice out front, leading, imitating you might at first think a woman's voice, but yearning to go even higher, higher than any person, woman or man's voice, higher and not break, not cry as he listens, as he hears the words crying almost and sings them, too, and almost weeps, and the words almost breaking his heart and he can't say why, as words repeat, repeat again, asking to be written down, put on a page as his voice repeats and echoes nothing he remembers exactly except it's there in the song, and he wants it here, too, him there and here too. Words, lyrics of a song sweetly breaking his heart because it's him, too, singing. As if in some indecipherable fashion he's remembering. Filling a page, filling in emptiness of lost years.

Later, he reads various stories about the song. A machine tells them, despite the fact it's just as memoryless as he is on his bad days. Empty tubes and wires, empty as a mirror and equally endlessly, tirelessly lying in wait, ready to reflect, to invent endless, tireless word after word to fill unfillable blankness of a screen, a flattened, bloodless surface with surfeits of words, including also black-and-white photos, multicolumns of print, full-colored scenes from movies unseen, unmade, disappearing faster than they appear, the way things seem also to work for him, more and more these days, him trying to make up stories with words from an unimaginably dense immensity of words, forests of words, deserts of words, of forgetting, of nothing there, only words from which any moment now he fears he soon won't be able to dredge up even his own name. Or name of the little street, little *impasse,* where he and a woman, his wife for twenty-three years, live half the year now in France.

Falsetto yearning, so high-pitched, unnatural you fear for the singer, pity him, picture him as he was photographed once upon a time, a small, slight man standing out front, separated slightly from the group of other young men (who, by coincidence probably, happened to call themselves Bluejays when they were recorded in 1953 on the Checker label), a record released during the year he was twelve, or during the next year when he's thirteen, or the next, his fourteenth year on earth, somewhere along in there is when he first heard ". . . bluebirds . . . just you wait and see," and he did wait and wait till finally one cute little lady from Harlem boarded for the summer with her grandfather while her grandfather was a boarder in his grandma's house, and love sparks between that little Harlem visitor and him, love at first sight and last sight and then out of sight far, far too soon, though never forgotten, forgiven, a girl who loved him back he was certain, at least she loved him, she did, she did, he's sure until and maybe even after she was pirated by a guy twenty-five years his senior up the block from Grandma, a guy with a nice car who could take the girl nice places and offer her oodles of nice things, offer much more to love than a lovesick teenage boy could offer a New York City kind of grown-up, light brown skin visitor who was the first ever to push down her panties and let him see, let him touch, let him stick his thingy in her thingy down there till his thing would shudder and almost ready to holler and sprout before swiftly she would arch her back, buck her narrow hips, her voice seething, "Huh-uh, huh-uh, no, no, babyboy," while strong as a python squirming, slithering away, him left to dangle, to spatter or spot with the calmest, shiny, tiny of puddles, her bare belly, bare thigh, and once he spots his grandmother's couch, though not to worry the girl smiled, wiping clean the cellophane-like slipcover wrapping the couch from the day the men delivered it till the day Grandma lay resting in peace beside it to greet mourners, too soon, too soon gone, like the Harlem girl, like Emmett Till, that Emmett Till down in Mississippi, fourteen like him when he's murdered and ain't never coming back, not Emmett Till, not the cute, cute, small person from Harlem, no, she never returns either, no joy and laughter and peace that the White Cliffs song promised, no laughter, just tears ever after, betraying, turning ass-backwards the song's happy lyrics, happy promise of a happy ending tomorrow, just you wait and see, and he does, he waits, listening to the song in his head, or barely audible in the staticky sputtering of local radio station WHOD's weak signal, or maybe on megawatt WLAC from Nashville broadcasting Randy's late nite R&B show nationwide.

He watches slicked-back guys in an old video. Sees Bluejays in their identical tuxes, identical postures in a cover photo for their freshly pressed Checker disk, their movements meticulously choreographed, synchronized to respond precisely on time, on the beat, though showmanship won't save the high tenor, naked inside the same shiny suit the others wear, save him from sure fall and pain when his voice, no matter how much purity and sweetness it brews, how high it climbs, must surely break, break before it brings his lady, brings mine, yours, anyone's lost lady love back, though if you could listen as he listens you must hear her in this song of yearning, of losing her or never having her, the sweetness of neither or both all at once in the music. Sorry for himself, sorry he is no bluebird in a flight of bluebirds or bluejays hovering over white cliffs, no blue bird without memories of falling and pain and memories of weeping for himself and sweetness of once soaring over white cliffs of Dover, cliffs he cannot recall though he must have viewed them numerous times crossing the Channel back and forth between England and France by ferryboat, no chunnel yet, not for another thirty, mostly forgotten years, thirty-plus years he learns because he looks up chunnel, among other never-ending reams of things, as if it might help him to remember correctly (or maybe incorrectly or help him invent) a visit to a lady he believed would always be waiting for him across those cold channel waters, a lady from Istanbul whose face he cannot recall and loved during his years as a Rhodes Scholar at Oxford.

CONCLUSIONS

Though he is, you are, and the known and unknown world are works in progress, the man has reached, or perhaps it's more precise to say that he has *formed* certain conclusions. Despite the fact he is not able to cite unimpeachably reliable sources to support or verify his conclusions, he believes he must strive or at least make a serious effort to explain the torn, spinning, ever-changing, unreliable work in progress he feels he is. Lost and found, he fears. A detached leaf twisting, blown flying in a storm.

Knowing beforehand the undependability of any conclusion he's able to reach or form, he often wonders why he struggles to arrive at a place he does not believe exists. A place—even if only for a moment—that might make a bit more sense of the unreasonable, unfathomable place in which he finds himself. Why would he suppose such a liberating place attainable? Or believe he would know what to do next if he arrived there. Unless he starts with the conclusion that contradictions and chaos of the life he lives are resolvable. But why should that be so. The idea that resolution might be possible is only another conclusion he could invent. Unsupportable, of course. A conclusion he picks out of thin air. Why start there with a make-believe fragment as insubstantial, as unreliable as he is, you are, as this known and unknown world.

All his conclusions starting and leading nowhere, except where he's stranded already, here where reasoning and logic struggle futilely. Nowhere. Conclusions enter a churning vastness beyond immense. A void beyond empty. Beyond filling. No work, no progress therein. Only what he might pretend is work or progress.

He comes to conclusions anyway. Sticking them into chaos. Stuck with them. Stuck with the language he speaks and writes as he attempts to organize memories, render memory as words. But persons, places, things that the man experiences remain imprisoned within time, locked up by time. Words seek to embody memories, but since language consists of noise and memories of memories, it remains time's slave. Produces only disembodied persons, places, things.

Words are memories that render for him the same service, the same illusion that the idea of a moment renders for time: the illusion that words can capture time, unveil time's secrets. But the man knows his memories and moments create only a fragile present tense. Mysteries intervene. Open always between his experience of one moment, one memory and the next. And he must go there. Goes there no choice, to the next moment, next memory, goes there before he knows there, and then it's gone, too. Gone before and after he gets there. Whatever he experiences gone, gone, gone—and he finds himself in a tangle he cannot grasp nor exit.

Pain that is not a word throbs in his shoulders, awakens him each morning. Some mornings it shivers down through one arm or the other and he makes a fist, flexes and unflexes his fingers, shaking them as if they have holes in their tips to drain hurt. He tries to remind himself that at his age he should be grateful for any alarm clock that still wakes him.

Problem with words may be, he concludes, that each of his words, any word, all words are as singular as every moment of time. What seems to be repetition of a word does not produce exactly a word previously heard or read or written or spoken or dreamed. Experiencing a word means internalizing that word, and each person's experience of any word is thus a specific, unique event. Happens only once. Present only once, he concludes. Room cleared only once for a word to be what it is. A word the same word yet different on every occasion it appears. Just as each passing moment occupies all time. Every moment creating time only for itself, and remains eternally isolated. Alone. Unique. One of a kind. Each word, like each moment of time, announces itself and its disappearance simultaneously. Words here and gone like wind, like time, like him, like you, he concludes.

Two words—*life* and *sentence.* Many meanings for either one. More if you stick the words together to signify one thing. But neither word alone nor both side by side fits the silent, implacable space he inhabits. Wherever or whatever it may be. The enigma of where he always is (or so it seems). And so must be.

Her show begins each morning as she opens those beautiful eyes. Or more likely, in this dream of her he's fashioning to steal a glimpse of her, of her show, of her dream, it begins before her beautiful eyes open. Her show on the screen behind her shut eyelids where sleep fades lazily, reluctantly, sleep not reigning exactly, yet not deposed either, by what's coming next, and then whatever, wherever, however, etc., the show she will watch begins, begins at a particular moment like this moment on this particular morning the man lies half-asleep himself, trying to imagine her life, her distant life—a moment in her life as separate from him as awake is separate from sleep, night from day, black from white, yes from no—her life that drifts so far from his and abandons him here, at the edge of extinction while she chooses from among many, many mysterious choices, but on each occasion, again and again—whether her choice conscious or unconscious, on purpose or not—when finally the choice, the urge to open her eyes prevails again, her choice, her eyes will have already marginalized him, her beautiful eyes seeking, seeing, and concentrating always on a show, a life from which he disappears, her show projected on a miniature screen like the screen on the iPhone lying on the night table beside her bed she will soon reach out for, lift, activate, and begin to study.

The privilege of seeing the beautiful space you live in is enough to keep me forever in love with you. Though I know that inside that space, you are not beautiful. He said those words once to the woman. And believed they might keep her. Believed he believed the words. Though she didn't. Though they absolutely were true. Like the bag he needs to pack.

When the man was a boy, the man murdered another boy. The murdered boy's age sixteen when he died, sixteen the age of the man when he was a boy and killed another boy. Sixteen an age the man who murdered a boy could not remember very well now, because every time he sits and tries to remember sixteen, his first thought always it had never happened, he'd never been a boy of sixteen who killed a boy of sixteen. Why would he, why would anyone do such a terrible thing, the man he was now asked himself. This other self he seemed he must be today, this being who he is, an old man lying awake or sitting on the edge of his cot and wondering how, why.

Sixteen a lost age. He recalls almost nothing about sixteen. Except a dead dead boy's face in a bed in a dark room staring at him. Asking *why* in the language of dark's dead silence.

"The reports of my death are greatly exaggerated," Mark Twain cabled to an NYC journalist after obituaries of Twain, who at the time was lecturing in Europe, were published in America in 1897.

Twain (aka Samuel Clemens) still alive three years later in 1900 (he doesn't die till 1910) and he reports from France his mixed reactions to the gigantic world's fair aka the Exposition Universelle in Paris. A fair organized to showcase and celebrate human progress as the nineteenth century ended and the twentieth century began. Humankind's inevitable, continuing progress, the sponsors of the fair proclaimed, progress guaranteed by myriad stupendous achievements in science and art that the fair showcases. Though the fair took place in France, historians also identify that event, coming as it does at the end of Queen Victoria's long, momentous reign (she was crowned 1838, died 1901), as the zenith of the British Empire's dominance as a world power, the threshold of the era called "modern" in which chaos and war will reign and Victoria's Britannia no longer rule the waves.

There must have been many boys sixteen years old alive during the fair's tenure. All of them dead now. How many of those sixteen-year-old boys killed other sixteen-year-old boys. Or how many sixteen-year-old girl killers of sixteen-year-old girls experienced the fair's magical electric lights blink and shimmer and shiver. Or how many cross-gender murders committed by sixteen-year-olds. Or murders of elders, child murders by sixteen-year-olds. All the perpetrators of murders during the fair's reign dead now, the man guesses. All the victims dead, too. So who to ask why, how.

They make love to each other. Back and forth, back and forth, until both are exhausted. Some of the work he performs to excite her and excite himself is conscious. He intends to do this or do that, and graphic words for his intentions may guide him, express a notion of what his body desires to give or take from her body and his body, except mostly he's beyond performing work, and not conscious of words because the back-and-forth connects, consumes, and frees both lovers, frees them from words anybody's ever thought of or carried around in their heads as something they might want to do to another person, like certain words in his head, words he believed were directing him to do to her this or that thing, in one particular way or another, but then all words dissolve, he dissolves, surprises himself as he becomes someone else, or something else altogether he never possessed words for, plans to become, he's doing with her, this lover, something else in terms he never could have imagined or worked his way towards, or performed, or put in words until it's her, her and him, both of them plunging and responding together, connected beyond understanding how and why, and the wordless back-and-forth speeds up incredibly, rapidly, slows down, back-and-forth, until no difference between them, it's not her, not him, everything is different, no distance between them, and what they are sharing reveals itself simply as unbelievably, undeniably what it is, a flow of revelations like those parts, those angles, those details of her naked body he had never noticed, never dreamed till back-and-forth shows them there and there they are, and he looks at her as he never looked before and knows he will never see her again nor anyone else ever see her again precisely as she is at this moment passing incalculably faster than seconds pass, and much more slowly, too, because there she is, she's absolutely real, not waiting to be discovered, she's there forever after and there forever before he would ever have believed possible, his discoveries of this and that about her body real and unreal as his death will be when he discovers it. Unreal, real as work he performs, as his words when they make love together.

The conclusion of the Board of Executive Clemency is to revoke probation and keep you in prison to serve the remaining years of your life sentence.

It will never conclude for us, announced the victim's father, speaking for all members of his family at a press conference. The idea of closure, of mercy, of forgiveness strike me almost as sick jokes, he said, given God's stern commandments to his chosen people—eye for an eye, tooth for a tooth. A monster ended my son's life. A monster guilty of an inexcusable crime. A monster that should have been executed thirty years ago. But he begged for mercy, begged for life. Though he showed no mercy the night he murdered my son. Where was mercy that terrible night. How can we be expected to forget or forgive. What good would mercy for my son's killer do now for my family or do for my dead son. And it's about him, my son, isn't it. Justice for him. For us. Not for an animal who murdered him. I sighed with relief, thanked God, took a deep breath and smiled, when I heard the Board announce its conclusion to lock up my son's killer forever.

This cell I am in, this cell in me of iron, stone, and steel, and no exit, my eternal, immortal cell lifts and floats free as it must always be, free of itself, free of its small understandings of itself, of what and where I seem an instant to be, the moment that seems to hold me, until instantly, I am not there inside it, though the guard passing by to check on me sees a cell that tells him I am exactly where I should be, sees my cage full not empty, and confirms his cell is full, too, occupied by him as his cell passes by mine, passing many, many other cells he sees and doesn't see are empty, empty as echoes of his footsteps dying, echoing against iron, stone, and steel that incarcerate and separate us, and blind the guard's gaze.

No name change for me, please. I will happily RIP Jacob. One name on my stone enough. If murderers get a stone. Jacob or Jake enough name. More than enough name. More than enough shame. Why add a family name or include a father's father's given name given to me at birth to identify me. Names to pin me down. Recall me. Convict me. Bury me.

As if any point of view might assemble all the fragments. As if something has been broken, not something fixed.

My father told me they climbed to the top of the Eiffel Tower. Said the view high up there of Paris spreading out quite a trip, but he preferred the boat ride down below on the Seine. Love boat, he smiled. Just enough of a smile for me to share, not envy, not be jealous of the boat ride's charm, the quiet, private, once-upon-a-time intimacies shared with a woman, my mother, my father's smile recalls, recalling the river's steady pull, night cloaking them, electric lights maybe not as stunning as they must have been during the 1901 Paris fair, but stunning still, illuminating elegant stacks of buildings that climb from black water edging both banks of the Seine, my father gliding along in the dark with my mother in another country when she was still alive and they still loved one another, his father told him, promised him, enough love sometimes to be very happy together.

In a cell you can watch the game. Turn your tiny TV to hoop. Players behind bars, in a box like you. Back and forth, up and down the court. Flying feet. Bodies in the air. Watch when your raggedy TV works, anyway. When you are free to watch. To fly. Float. Score. Win.

He reads, reads all the time and learns that a man of color or rather a man some human beings who consider themselves the man's betters, designate as colored, as if their own skin color invisible, a colorlessness that they designate as white to distinguish themselves unmistakably and eternally from colored inferiors like the man of color, Lewis Howard Latimer, whose inventions, experiments, and business acumen during his long association with Thomas Alva Edison, the reader learns, were crucial to the development, commercialization, and proliferation of the electric light bulb as the twentieth century dawned, and the man who reads that story wonders if Lewis Howard Latimer, son of a woman and man enslaved in Virginia, attended the Paris fair.

My heart like needles ever true
Turns to the maid of ebon hue

I love her form of matchless grace
The dark brown beauty of her face.

(Lines he reads from one of Latimer's poems collected and published by his daughters)

She is naked while she phones and orders a pizza. Decides to stay naked. A big surprise for the delivery guy when she opens her door. Bigger surprise when she hands him a camcorder and invites him to film her posing naked on her bed. A sure enough show for the pizza guy, and the video of him videoing the pretty young woman's energetic, X-rated display of her intimate parts surely got the attention of three or four inmates assigned to work in the prison laundry room who gathered round to peek over the shoulder of a fellow inmate who allows them to watch the latest porn he's checking out on his mobile phone, one of those lucky inmates who could afford the sky-high price of a phone, the price of the privilege of access and the opportunity to operate that piece of contraband inside prison walls, though both possession and use of a mobile phone absolutely forbidden by prison rules. For a rare moment, one of the lucky ones chooses to share—for a quick minute anyway—his good fortune that the others dream of and envy, often to the point of hating fellow prisoners who own the power to exercise powers ordinary inmates understand no way they will ever manage to negotiate or buy or steal. The bunched-up group in the laundry room stares, more or less silently, absorbed by full-frontal views of a naked woman's crotch between her spread-eagled legs, side views, views of her from behind as she crouches on her knees to elevate and wiggle a firm, trim butt, and though not exactly transfixed—some guys grunt, sigh, mutter, exclaim, wag their heads—a literally captive audience, except for the one man who looks away from the brightly colored, HD-quality images streaming across the screen, a man whose eyes stray to deliver their attention elsewhere, a not-lasting-very-long absence—he doesn't want to miss too much—though no doubt, riding along where his eyes take him, he travels for an immeasurable instant to an impossibly distant place before he reenters the party in the prison laundry room and returns the pretty young thing's naked smile.

BLACK TEARS

(I)

You are inside. Inside yourself. And often you want out. But no way out. No matter how desperate or cunning you happen to be, you are inside yourself and can't get outside. Except perhaps by dying. Ceasing to be. D-ceased. Outside not inside a life.

But if no longer alive inside yourself, where are you. What would you be. Who. To whom would death announce its presence and your absence. If no consciousness of yourself inside yourself, where would you be. Or not be. Who would know. If no *you* inside keeping track, what's the difference between inside and outside. And wouldn't losing the ability to tell the difference between inside and outside extinguish the difference. Bring on madness. Annihilation of yourself.

To be, it seems you need someone inside you, conscious of you. Someone trapped forever inside. You can't get outside yourself without dying. Without madness. Without performing a fatal act of separation.

Trying to get outside yourself may be no less difficult, no less impossible, than attempting to understand death. We know very little, and that little amounts, probably, to less than nothing, about death. Nothing beyond its certainty, beyond our fear and loathing, our magical thinking, wishful thinking that despite death's inevitability, somehow it may spare the voice inside.

Time a measure of a person's distance from death, but since time as mysterious as death, the how, why, and what time measures is incomprehensible. We say time passes and say life passes, as if words unveil a connection or perhaps the disconnect of death and time. But unlike an individual live person, time does not pass away. Time fills lives and empties them simultaneously.

Death one undetachable moment from the moments the voice inside us tries to keep track of, tries to make sense of. Not separation from time. We are always and forever immersed in time. Or it immerses us. Our tears, perhaps, the closest we come to understanding time. How a part inside you surrenders, separates, and then seems not you. Seems to have escaped into a world outside of you. You and not you. Lost in an alien world. Where your tears, sweat, piss, shit go. Going, going. Gone. No longer inside you. Your excesses, excretions. You once, then not you.

And doesn't that rot, stink, excess preserve as well as remove part of you with it when it's expelled. Take you with it. You no longer inside yourself. Something of you released. Scattered witnesses from inside you outside you. Though insensate, mute, blind. Confirming a different you, another you. Gone. To some unspeakably different place. Free at last, perhaps. Practice, preparation, preview, maybe, of death's inevitable release of everything inside you. For all of you, including the voice inside that talks to you, to vanish and disappear, to become irretrievably what's outside. A release after perplexing incarceration. Termination of what seemed a life sentence inside, a perpetual stalemate. Until it resolves itself as simply, as irresistibly, as undignified, as necessary, as final as a bowel movement or urination.

(II)

I don't remember either, don't remember anybody in the podcast saying black tears, my sister says. But I know what Mommy meant when she said black tears to you, my sister continues. And I bet you are feeling it, too. Or should be. Mom could get things absolutely right. She had that deep understanding about some things, things that truly mattered. Like her absolute love for us, no questions asked, love she gave each of us, everyday, no questions asked, nothing missing, nothing none her kids had to beg for or bargain for. She was yours. You were hers. No separation. You know how she was. And no getting around her when she hits you with something she truly believes.

A son forty-four years in prison. Then a grandson in another prison over thirty years. And a nice person comes along talking about how awful. What a terrible situation. For Mom. For her son and grandson and all the rest of us out here suffering. Podcast talking like talking is suffering, too. That's what Mom's telling you. Them talking like talk comes closer, brings them closer to us, this nice person who's doing most the talking and all the other people nice like her listening maybe, and the un-nice ones closer, too, even those voices in the podcast sending us to hell and good riddance, all of those voices supposed to be coming closer, coming at us, but truth is they talking to themselves, and Mom, you, me, all us supposed to sit and listen like the talk about us, not them.

All that talking and talking and them not one measly inch closer really 'cause they still think Moms' tears black and their tears not. Their tears couldn't be black because then they'd be across a line they ain't never crossing.

That's what mom saying to you or you putting in her thoughts, or you should be putting in her thoughts. Black tears what she would have heard them saying if she was still around to listen to a podcast.

I hear them talking about tears, Mom be saying to you. And she woulda said, Many, many times, till the day I died (not *died*—wrong verb tense I quickly, quietly correct my sister, my Mom—not dead, not gone yet), many times I surely shed tears. Tears for my son, Mom says, then tears for your son, my grandson, tear after tear, but none that crying brought son or grandson back home. Whole lots and lots of tears, and not one them tears black. Never saw a black tear. Mine nor nobody else's.

Black tears what they talking about. Other people's tears. Should know better, but maybe they can't help talking the way they do. Other people's suffering and crying. Not suffering and crying of the ones talking. Their words say no. Not us. Tears and talking not about us. Nothing to do with us. The line always there, Mom hears those podcast voices good and evil declare the line always here, always there and same voices say we ain't hardly dumb bunnies enough to hop over it. Damned sure ain't never gone risk nothing precious to cross it. Not today. Not tomorrow. Your mama hears the line they ain't crossing in all that podcast talking. Mom hears them sorry about black tears and knows hers not black.

Podcast ended many minutes ago. Last episode of six and now I'd listened to all of them. Mom fades. Then my sister, too, dissolves in the long silence in this room after the podcast concludes, and I'm alone. The entire series clearly sympathetic and fair toward my son's side of events. Identifying with him, casting a positive, compelling light on his years of troubles: of illness, of struggle, of remorse for taking a life, his determination to do the best he could under the mind-and-body crushing circumstances imposed by incarceration in an adult maximum security prison while still an adolescent, then locked up three more decades while striving to transform himself into a trustworthy, valuable person able to contribute positively to society. Podcast also clearly exposed the cruelty and injustice of the way he'd been treated by Arizona's Board of Executive Pardons and

Parole. Podcast documents time and time again in grim detail how the odds purposely stacked against him. Illuminates the wonder of his survival as a decent human being. Greater wonder of a man who remains after nearly thirty-five years in prison, unwaveringly committed to helping others survive the enduring, toxic forces constructed to destroy them, destroy him.

Then talking ends. It's over. All six podcast episodes played out. Followed by silence.

Alone again now. I let go of mother, sister. No space for them in this utter silence, and I try to spare them the weight of it. Try to spare myself the weight of their absence. Weight of this silence I must bear without them. Silence until I'm ready to listen again to voices the podcast records. Waiting for them to speak. To break the silence. To color or not color a tear I will or will not shed for a son if I listen once more.

RIP

William Henry Sheppard, a man of partly African descent, born in Virginia towards the end of the nineteenth century, became a Presbyterian missionary and lived twenty years in Africa before he returned to America and died in Kentucky in 1927, and sometimes I talk to him the way I talk to you, Bro. Ask him questions about his life to help me make sense of mine. Recently, I shared the good news with WHS that you, Rob, my youngest brother, my only surviving male sibling, have been released from prison after serving forty-four years of a life sentence.

Told WHS that twenty-nine years ago, while you were still locked up, your son Omar was murdered. During my brother's incarceration, I tell Sheppard, my brother fathered a second son, and that son named Chance because no conjugal visits legal in PA prisons, and thus a very small chance, indeed, conception might occur in the random, rare twenty-five to thirty minutes of privacy a couple could beg or bribe a guard to provide. Chance his first name and Mandela his second name. Named Chance Mandela because not only did my brother's son manage to get conceived, he also chose to be born the very day Nelson Mandela released after twenty-three years in a

South African prison. And I tell WHS that Chance Mandela, my youngest brother's son, my nephew, and half brother of Omar, has just sent me a beautiful photo of himself, his wife, and their infant son they named Josiah Omar.

So it goes on this slaveroad. I admire the family photo. Touched by it. Recall Rebekah's family—the Prottens, R and her spouse Christian and their daughter Anna Maria smiling in a family portrait painted three centuries ago by Johann Valentin Haidt. Christian Jacob Protten, R's husband, the troubled father of his family, our soul brother, Bro, yours and mine, and Sheppard's. Protten who shares the name Jacob with my imprisoned son.

Protten of mixed African and European descent. As was his wife, Rebekah. Both of them Moravian missionaries, travelers, wanderers who spent time in Europe, the West Indies, Africa. Christian Jacob Protten born in Africa, educated in Europe, returning after decades abroad to serve as teacher and chaplain at Fort Christiansborg on the West African coast. A scholar, a published author and translator, one of the first to transcribe Ga and Fanti so that those languages could be read and written as well as heard. Protten also a philanderer, notorious drunk, punished for his immoral behavior by a Presbyterian Church that turned a blind eye on the fact that the slave trade supplied most of its African converts. His European colleagues considered Protten a dreamer. Too full of arrogance, self-conceit. Like Sheppard, two centuries later, he was praised, denounced, hounded because too colored or not colored enough for those who deemed him colored.

And so it seems to go. Eternally. On and on. Lives on a slaveroad crossing the Atlantic. Lives and deaths our families endure. Lives and deaths and stories, like yours, Bro, that sear, brand, fill me with love, remorse, shame, anger, pride, a longing to be in many places, many times, many bodies, carried away with them, returning here to find they have never left, never gone away, not waiting somewhere for me to come join them, but here where I'm with them, here where I speak to them and yearn for them to speak.

On and on. Like the day I encounter drippy purple letters spelling *RIP Omar* scrawled in the top left corner of a frozen puddle of paint that stands upright so it's like a gate or door, an eight-foot-tall, ten-foot-wide puddle of graffiti on a black metal canvas within the gray metal frame situated in front of a steel barrier and iron-railed fence where the pedestrian walkway across Williamsburg Bridge divides. *RIP Omar* appearing there where I must choose, if I intend to proceed beyond the movie screen of embedded graffiti, to go either right or left. Either a double-lane ramp designated for foot traffic or on the other lane designated for bikes. At that juncture in the walkway approximately a fifth of the way across Williamsburg Bridge if you start at Delancey Street, where I do, you may discover as I did *RIP Omar* freshly painted on a placard erected a century ago by the city of New York's Department of Bridges. A memorial the department intended to celebrate and commemorate completion of a monumental undertaking, the construction of the Williamsburg Bridge, but serving now as a billboard for any scribbler who decides to paint or tag or splash or inscribe or illustrate or decorate or deface it with piss or spit or shit or whatever, adding another layer to the many, many impacted layers that bury the memorial's original embossed letters deeper and deeper.

Me thinking when the message *RIP Omar* appears first time on Williamsburg Bridge that I need you, my youngest brother, here, and thinking he is here, on this bridge, as I think of him and try to think what he might be thinking as each brother nods silently to himself and nods at the other, thinking, *No*, not RIP . . . no, no . . . never . . . never RIP. Nodding no—no, as if each brother's long, long thought visible to the other, endured by the other while we nod. Nodding no, never. Not gone yet. Do not rest in peace, Omar. Not now, not here on this metal gate, this painted door of no return encountered, passed by while crossing the Williamsburg Bridge. It nods at us and we nod and perhaps stare back at it, but the door, the gate never quite opens or closes, it nods quietly, forever, without movement, always neither open nor shut except if two brothers daydream it could or should connect what's already over and done to whatever comes next.

Connect us, please, we are thinking, I think. Connect us to the Empire of Omar. No empire ever rests in peace, does it. Although each and every one falls. *Requiescat in pace*. Three Latin words whose initial letters, RIP, are imported into English, and translated in English vernacular as *rest in peace*. The letters *RIP* carved on European tombstones begin to appear from about the eighth century onwards. For speakers of English *rip* also a verb meaning to cut, tear apart, or tear roughly away. Or a noun: something that results from being torn or split apart. Omar a Muslim name signifying "flourishing, long-lived." Like the caliph Umar (634–44), instrumental in the rise of Islam. *Umr* an Arabic word for life. Average life expectancy seventy-six years for an Omar born in the USA in 2004. My youngest, last live brother's son Omar, born 1972, died 1993. How many years ripped from Omar's life expectancy by a hail of assassins' bullets. *Om* considered by many ancient philosophical texts to be the sound of the universe, all other sounds carried within it. In Sanskrit *om* called Pravana, and means to hum, a hum considered unlimited and eternal.

But can a black boy be an empire. An emperor. Are black boys assassinated or simply offed, executed, murdered, lost, wasted, blown away.

Each person, each of us greedy, relentless as empire. Each empire greedy, relentless as a person. Empire consumes people. People consume empires. Roman. Chinese. Turkish. Portuguese. American. Dahomean. Gold Coasts. Slave Coasts. Elmina. Are empires doors of no return.

I rendezvoused once with Omar at the big Sears department store in East Liberty that used to take up a whole block of Highland Avenue, not far from Peabody, my old high school also on Highland Avenue. School gone now like Sears. Peabody High, where our sports teams were Highlanders, our logo a guy in a skirt playing a bagpipe, Highlanders a lame-ass, embarrassing name compared to Bulldogs, our nasty archrivals at Westinghouse High. Back home in the Burg paying a visit from my empire in Philly, empire of comfortable town house in a row of town houses adjacent to green Clark Park near Penn's campus, my first marriage still intact, my university teaching job with its perks and status and security and salary and copious time off basically unfathomable to my mostly barely scuffling by or worse relatives I loved but whom I didn't want to think about too much, couldn't think very much about because I'd have to admit and cope with the vast distance between us that had gradually become unfathomable for me, but clearly, that early September with me home a couple days until my fall semester duties commenced, clearly, since next to impossible for anyone else in the immediate family to find the money quickly, legally, thus clearly, no doubt about it, my turn to buy Omar a winter coat.

And clearly a stranger to my nephew Omar, who takes a while to raise his eyes from the sidewalk or whatever it is he studies down there between the cracks instead of meeting my gaze. Especially when I try speaking directly to him. Soft brown eyes like yours, my brother, like mine, my eyes Omar scrupulously avoids as I avoid long, hard looks at my Pittsburgh people. Which one of us a stranger, a grown-up, which one an irrelevancy to the other. Him large for his age, man size at thirteen—growing . . . growing . . . gone. Sleeves of jacket he wears expose wrists, I bet. Om already prowling, I guessed, to make his way in that darkness, that labyrinth, that limbo he must enter to escape Omar, earn Omar, own Omar.

Winter coat or jacket or both purchased that day for Omar. Boy needed both, didn't he. And I could afford both, couldn't I. Afford more. Ashamed to pretend otherwise. Ashamed in the eyes of my family if I could or couldn't. Wouldn't my three kids be wearing good winter coats when wind howled and snow fell in Philly. Does winter in Philly ever swirl and almost blow you over the way it used to kick butt in that wind tunnel of Highland Avenue after we crossed Penn Avenue fall and winter, when I, then my brothers and sister humped daily to Peabody High to save bus fare nobody could afford. A long way round, school a million miles away maybe, but worth it, our mother said, said anything better, she said, than that lousy rat-trap worthless ignoramus Westinghouse High she'd attended her own self back in the day when they at least taught students penmanship, the neat, legible hand she still possessed.

Your father and me breaking our behinds to keep us in this neighborhood, on this street, crowded up in this teensy house so you all can go to Peabody, but worth it if you all do right and get your education, she said. But Om never heard Mom preach and fuss at us. Really no choice anyway for Omar. Born and raised in Homewood, in Hazelwood. No choice but Westinghouse High. Never got out the hood, out those Homewood, Hazelwood woods you could say if you had nothing nicer to say and trying to be funny.

But Om not wild like me, my brother once mused to me after Omar gone. Mom having a fit the whole time, but I loved the year after we moved from Shadyside and I had to go to Westinghouse, my brother said. Loved those crazy House niggers, loved the crazy nigger in me when I was in the House. Stone dug the House till I got myself too busy smoking, making money, and had to quit-u-ate my ass outta there. But Om. Om just did his time. Never in no bad trouble. Least none I knowed about. None but the little bits I remember his mom cried over when she visited me. Seem like Omar walked into Westinghouse High School one morning and four years later Omar walked out. Didn't bother nobody. No teachers on his case. Nobody bothered him. Cept maybe couple them fresh, pesty girls claiming he the daddy.

No education about it. But what you expect. House same as House always been. You sit there neat and quiet four years, mouth shut, minding your own business, they give you that paper and off you go. Ain't learned shit, but shit, street's gon teach you soon enough. Teach you to be a fool, if you a fool like me. But Om different. Needed a different me. And swear to God it hurts me, breaks my heart and hurts me more than I can say and wouldn't even try to say, big Bro, cept I know you already know how goddamned, pitiful sorry I am I wasn't around, wasn't that different person poor Om needed. Om be alive today maybe. Daddy to them little kids he left behind. Grown-ups now I tries my best to keep up with since I been out the joint but getting too goddamn old.

One miracle is that despite forty-four years of imprisonment, you, the youngest of my three brothers, remember freedom. I believe nobody grants a person freedom. A person must remember freedom. How did you, how do you remember, lil Bro.

How does Omar. How does he stay alive, I am wondering as I get close as I can to the letters of his name, close to someone's wish that Omar rest in peace slap-dashed here of all places, here in New York City, where of all places I find myself one day and find myself needing to approach a tombstone taller than me, tombstone of steel and paint surprising me so much first time I see it bearing Omar's name and RIP, I had to lower my eyes and pass by in silence, concentrate on going either right or left on Williamsburg Bridge because the walkway divides, and if you want to reach the walkway's termination in Williamsburg, you must choose one way or the other after you have traversed perhaps a fifth of the bridge's length and find yourself here where anonymous officials, all probably white men in suits, all probably dead by now, chose to plant a black steel placard framed within gray steel of the bridge's steel soil to mark and memorialize completion of a task they'd been assigned, a formidable piece of work accomplished, not necessarily destined to last forever, they probably knew, though lasting, they probably understood, perhaps a good while longer than they would, and perhaps that possibility a bit satisfying for dead people once oblivion swallows them, but on the other hand, perhaps they would be very surprised to see the bridge today, unsettled maybe by the volume of streaming traffic beneath the walkway, new skylines of towers, needles, mile after mile of hundred-acre-sized high-rise warrens in rows visible from up here, the ceaseless roar, and the officials might shyly—overwhelmed a bit by terror and incomprehension—drop their eyes and get on with whatever business occupies their time now, not exactly grateful and not exactly ungrateful either to have something else to do other than look surprised, stunned, unsettled as I was first time seeing my nephew suddenly appear here. My nephew shot and killed twenty years ago in Pittsburgh, Pennsylvania, on November 8, 1993, while his girlfriend, their baby in her arms, stood screaming at the top of stairs leading up to her apartment.

Omar appearing on Williamsburg Bridge, seeing him again, seeing Om, your son, my nephew, his name painted here, and me stunned and wondering, seeing your long-lost son's name, then seeing him, and seeing his name again next time I walked across the bridge, then once more, then painted over, but then slopped back on again, red instead of purple paint, in the same upper-left corner of a graffiti-coated metal canvas until one day I am driven to step closer, step to the very edge, where the walkway dead-ends before it divides, where a chin-high iron fence and ten-foot-tall steel barrier stand behind the steel-framed commemoration of the builders' success, there, here, I search, only inches from vastness of empty air beyond barrier and fence, gripping the fence while I inspect impacted layers of graffiti crusting a black steel cage. My foot braced, I lean over the memorial placard's edge, as close as I can get to it, free hand scraping off snow and ice and whatever else flakes away as I try to read whatever else might be there to read, whatever else is there along with Om, there like Om not resting in peace. Because Omar does not Rest In Peace, does he, my brother.

Too cold a February day for even my gloved fingers to dig very deep into layers of frozen paint, frozen iron, brass, steel. But a revelation received anyway up that close and personal to a wannabe tombstone, to a wannabe grave, to painted letters mourning and grieving as if no Omar anymore. Below the memorial's bottom edge, a gap of maybe a foot or so extends from one supporting leg of the placard to the other, and in this space, this gap, this opening below the placard you'd be unlikely to pay any attention to unless you happen to wind up precisely, precariously where I stand, the revelation of *Omar* is tagged atop a steel beam that connects the memorial's legs. Omar in white paint this time, a tiny, secret tag on a black steel beam, and then another tag and another and another, forever, tags far too small for eyes to see, invisible tags I read one after the other, then see him, see Omar, I see my nephew Om again.

Here's another one of my long thoughts you also may think, Bro. Freedom perhaps means a person has no choice but chooses anyway. Freedom an empire. Freedom the cell you are born in and die in. Freedom born when you are born, dies when you die. Imprisons you. Freedom here before you got here and here after you are gone. Freedom not you. Imprisons you, no choice. Freedom is not knowing why or how freedom imprisons. Freedom breathes only inside you, yet lives somewhere else not you that you can't understand. No one does. But no one's iron-barred cell emptied of freedom unless you forget freedom, and even forgotten, freedom's there still when you remember it. Freedom like the unsheddable mystery and burden of yourself.

I do not remember the winter coat Omar picked out from Sears nor remember how he looked in it. Do not remember if I bought him a jacket, too. Do remember Om liked the coat. Sure of that. Recall us both very pleased. Happy about the new coat. Om put it on and no matter what the weather outdoors, he wore the coat out of the store. Om carrying maybe a big Sears bag or big Sears box with his old, probably funky coat balled up in it.

Maybe we remember things, Bro, because too much always happening to remember so people make up stuff to pretend they don't forget. Guess that means you could say nothing happens unless there's a story about it and I guess that's what the Igbo mean by the proverb Chinua Achebe quotes in *Things Fall Apart*: all stories are true.

I found *Pittsburgh Post-Gazette* articles on the internet dated November 22 and 23, 1999, reporting that the last of the three men accused of shooting Omar at least five times in the head was found guilty finally of first-degree homicide six years after the murder. Another shooter, convicted and sentenced in April 1998, had been the one in a fight, a knock-down, drag-out fight with Omar in a Hazelwood bar, a fight the man was losing when the cops arrived to break it up, and he refused to cooperate with the cops, declaring, "Me and my boys will take care of it. What happens in the street stays in the street." Five hours later, around 1:30 a.m. November 8, 1993, Omar shot to death and three men in a car arrested fleeing the murder scene. Two of them are still serving life terms plus in prison. The third killed in a motorcycle accident just a few months after a jury acquitted him in 1998.

The *Post-Gazette* also reported that in 1993, the year in which Omar was shot, his half brother Jason had died a month earlier from a bullet in the brain, allegedly the result of a game of Russian roulette. Jason not your son, Bro, but did he ever accompany Om and their mom on her prison visits, Jason the son of a different father, but did he ever come to visit you in prison with his mother and his half brother, your son Omar.

The year 1993 set a record: 118 homicides in Allegheny County, so many the paper labeled 1993 "the Year of Death," and noted that black males, fifteen to twenty-four years old, comprised forty-six of the victims.

Thank you for the information, motherfucker, I say to the unlucky number 13 flashing at this exact moment on my iPad: 8:13 a.m.; March 3, 2022. Our mom so fearful of unlucky 13, she said, she had suffered three extra hours of agony holding me in so I'd be born on June 14, not 13. Thank you, I holler out loud at the iPad when I touch it to start it working, and 13 pops up this morning.

I often wonder and you must, too, my brother, how does Om's mom survive her double loss, her two sons ripped away in a single year. How does she suffer it, bear it, that intelligent, kind woman, that intelligent, wild, beautiful young girl you tell me you loved and who gave love back, you say. Puppy lovers, head over heels in love once when you all just babies, you said, and now a different love shared I've witnessed in her, in you, Bro. Love freeing the two of you to continue loving Omar together.

Of course, I scoured the internet after *RIP Omar* stopped me in my tracks on the bridge. No, *RIP Omar* didn't stop me in my tracks. The words assailed me. Sent me running for cover. And consequently, from dredging the internet, seeking more information or maybe seeking less, I learn the length, width, history, etc., of the Williamsburg Bridge, average number of suicides per year who leap from it, and I learn Willy B the name some locals call the bridge, and learn Michael Kenneth Williams—the actor who played Omar in *The Wire*—a homeboy, local hero born in Brooklyn, died of an overdose in Williamsburg.

So, Bro. Isn't it more than likely that it's him addressed—Michael Kenneth Williams. Mr. World-Famous Omar and not Omar my nephew, not Omar your son, and certainly not your new grandbaby I have met only once in a picture that his father, my nephew, emailed me. No. Huh-uh. Not our missing, lost, and found boys on that bridge, but Mister Michael Kenneth Williams the one whose pretend name Omar painted on the bridge. Wouldn't he, Bro, Michael Kenneth Williams, be the one up there dead and laid to rest, mourned by a grieving true fan: *RIP Omar.*

I imagine infant Omar lying on his belly wet and warm. The baby blinks. Or cries out once in its sleep. That quick. Quicker. Way quicker than outcry or blink, the slaveroad gone. Gone quick. Gone. Gone. Gone. Gone. Gone.

SISTER'S ATTIC

The attic of my sister. My sister's attic. Or say or call it the third floor, as my sister does sometimes still say, Up on the third floor, where for a while her fourth daughter stayed or boarded a few years anyway, as I recall, long enough to leave behind when she left lots of her stuff added to the stuff already stuffed up there on the third floor when occasionally, I guess you could say, seasonally, I return home to my family in Homewood, Pittsburgh, and find myself sleeping with lots of my niece's stuff, some packed, some not, scattered here and there among piles, stacks, boxes, shopping bags, suitcases, garment and dry cleaner bags hung, draped, packages, bundles, taped cartons, yellow manila envelopes, folders, shelves full, and wandering stuff squeezed, hidden, lost and found in my sister's attic, my sister's place for what she can't let go, generations of it, of our mom's stuff and stuff of mom's mom, etc., going way, way back, photo albums, record albums, old 45s, letters, notes, shoeboxes, clothes, books, lists, certificates certifying this and that and nothing, and my niece's stuff among the latest stuff stuffed and packed up there competing for the whatever small or none whatsoever space remains in a space tiny in the first place and still now so tiny I hesitate to call the space on the third floor a room and sometimes say or call her attic a closet when I'm teasing my sister and sometimes she smiles or occasionally cuts her eyes at me to reply to what she doesn't really find very funny, but the razor in her eyes is play sharp not deadly sharp as I am reminded by her in no uncertain terms I am her brother, an older brother she's known her whole life and she knows that sometimes he thinks he's funny, tries to be some kind of damned smart-aleck comedian or master of ceremonies, which definitely he is not, so she ignores or cuts her eyes, no harm no foul, you dumb bunny of a big stupid-ass big brother want to be funny and cute and I wouldn't hurt you for the world, my brother, but I could, mm-hmm, and don't you ever forget it, older brother of my life, brother who when he comes home stays up there where there's barely room for the small bed in which her last daughter, my niece, slept, *last* meaning daughter *born last* to my sister, last not meaning *only* daughter left alive, since surely, thank goodness, another daughter besides my niece who boarded in the attic is still alive, too, thus two alive, though two daughters dead when I sleep there now when I'm in town, up there in the attic of my sister, but not cramped for space in the least, truly happy and grateful to be home and to have a familiar place to lay my head once I mount the treacherous, for an old man, steep stairs to get up there above the other two floors of my sister's narrow house, house it seems leaning to one side when you first glance up at it from the window of a cab caught at the airport or train station, sister's house leaning to steady itself maybe, keep itself from slowly sliding back down from the crest of the steep hill it rides on North Graham Street, sister's house going quiet, going to sleep beneath me sleeping in the attic of my sister, welcome again, home again home again like my last-born, grown woman niece as long as it made sense for her to be or to stay up there in the attic, her, my niece with one sister alive, two dead, her sisters who arrived before she did, one of her dead sisters my sister's firstborn, living almost twenty-seven years, long enough to bear a child of her own, and my sister's second daughter still alive, thank goodness, but the third of my sister's daughters stayed only till she was not quite two years old, so my sister with two daughters here once, then gone, and two still here, the crowd of us all crowded into the tiny space up there in the attic, or the copious *spaces* up here, I guess you also could say, many spaces with plenty enough room for laughing, crying, being alone, poking around, lonely, fooling around, daydreaming, staring each night at the dark in the attic of my sister when I make it back home, the visits home scarcer and scarcer it seems these days, days aging faster than I do, it seems, I can barely keep up, days gone, gone, leaning in the wrong direction, and they have already slid away and I can't catch up though it seems like just yesterday, like it happened just yesterday as somebody in the family's reminding me about this or that thing somebody said or did or I find a sepia snapshot in the attic or maybe just dreamed it like I dreamed of three or four of the youngest generation, a gaggle of them but few enough, or me with hands enough to clasp each by the hand as I lead them, guide them up steep stairs climbing to the attic of my sister, her attic where we all lie awake or sleeping perhaps already or pass each other on the narrow steep steps in the narrow stairwell with barely any room to get by and nothing on the close, bare plaster walls to hold on to so I grasp each of the hands, all of them boy hands for some reason this time in the dark on this specific evening that I am leading them up narrow steps to my sister's attic, Josiah Omar, Orion, Caleb, three of their names, three in particular for some unknown reason I pick out from multitudes of family names and name three of ours who are among those present now, naming them in reverse order of their recent births, youngest first, for some reason I do not know, but it works and the crew of them, the whole slew of them are behind me and with me and me with enough hands to go round somehow, I don't know how, but there, here we come hands interlocked mounting those attic stairs, a quiet gang nobody has to shush because we know somehow that the house we haunt sleeps silent as a ghost below us, around us, my sister's leaning, sliding house asleep *selah* as we climb and pass folks even in utter darkness we can tell they are there and they are our own quiet folks, reams and reams of them passed in less than the time a single moment, single step takes on the attic steps, our people brushing by, even closer, even faster, even in less time than any of us will ever understand, even beyond our hungriest imaginings of what has been or will be or might be, or what it might bring, things brushing past us that fast as those boys and I climb slowly up to my sister's attic and pass crowds of our folks coming down, going up those steep stairs, no light except the whisper of shoulders of passing crowds we nearly brush so close, close to them as a brush close to fingernails just before it paints them, the brush tipped with colored polish my sister's husband, Aaron, uses in his job at the funeral parlor where he drives the hearse and also grooms the nails of people's dearly beloved, even toenails for some reason sometimes, and my sister loves him deeply, as she often confides to me or sings to him, but never, never, she confides, could I ever hold those cold dead hands, let alone cold feet Aaron touches, not even to feed my family, no, no, no way, or who knows, no, no, or maybe, she says, and I listen and hear her, and I see them, woman, man, wives, husbands, children, more folks than I can count while I sleep in the attic of my sister.

AUTHOR'S AFTERWORD

There is no afterword. Nothing more to say. Nothing there. Nothing here. But to please myself, and perhaps for the sake of art, the sake of a nostalgic belief that writing can render those illusions of balance, symmetry, order, beauty, freedom that art attempts, I will add an author's afterword here. I will pretend to step outside of time again as I did in an author's forward. Pretending again, though I admit now, an author's afterword to *Slaveroad* serves no useful purpose. Serves only me. A foreword, an afterword only games, after all, literary tricks, pretending to stop time and make space for a story. But time neither opens nor closes, begins nor ends. Never yields. Though stories do.

And this one does end. And did not change the terrible things weeping through it. This story, this book yields like the dying bird in my front yard, the one I almost stepped on yesterday and shoveled up dead this morning onto a dustpan and tossed over the high backyard hedges into the green spaces no one owns behind my house.

But *Slaveroad* is a story that hasn't ended yet. It's here. Now. Where we are. What we are. A story compounded of stories told, retold, untold, not told. Stories repeating. Listened to or not listened to.

This fiction. This autobiography. Shall I try to sell this one. Though it fails. Must fail because it cannot clean up behind itself. Name itself.

Slaveroad beckons. Reigns still. Bodies accumulated upon it, whatever else they might be, remain bodies. My editor, who is also my friend, evaluates my words and, among other responses, some of them of incalculable value to me, offers what this story might be worth in dollars for me and for the publisher she represents. My literary agent, also my friend, receives the offer and asks me how we should proceed, and then she inquires almost apologetically (almost impishly) do I want this story, this manuscript (I also refer to as an "autobiography") to be considered as fiction or nonfiction while on its way to market, to market to be a book.

I listen and not listen. We all do. Here. Today. With no sad or happy ever-after on the way. Nor here now, nor coming once upon a time before. No stories. No autobiographies. No time. Only words spoken, words on the page. Until no words, no page, no author, no readers. Slaveroad teeming and empty as time always is. A slaveroad always. Capturing us, owning us once we are discarded and launched and floating and drowning, and on our way. Where. Here. Who we are. Then not.